Monica wasn't surprised when Derek took her hand. It seemed natural for friends, even new friends, to hold hands while walking around such a romantic place.

"Thanks a million for helping me with my English homework," Derek said softly. "I'm sorry we didn't get to your algebra."

"Oh, that's okay. I'm not having too much trouble with that," Monica said.

"Well, I wish I could repay you in some way. You really saved my life, helping with that report."

Monica didn't answer for a moment. All evening a bizarre idea had been growing in her mind, but she didn't even want to put it into words.

She looked at Derek and wondered how he would react. No, she couldn't even mention it.

Strangely enough, it was Derek who brought up the subject Monica had been avoiding all evening. "I know you'd like some help with your bars routine," he said matter-of-factly. "But that's something I can't help you with. I wish I could, though."

"Yes," Monica said slowly. "So do I."

If only you knew what I was thinking, she thought to herself. Her plan was crazy—dangerous, even.

But for all her determination to put it out of her mind, the idea wouldn't go away.

Other Fawcett Girls Only Titles

Breaking The Rules

PERFECT 10
2

HOLLY SIMPSON

FAWCETT GIRLS ONLY • NEW YORK

RLI: $\dfrac{\text{VL 6 \& up}}{\text{IL 7 \& up}}$

A Fawcett Girls Only Book
Published by Ballantine Books
Copyright © 1989 by Cloverdale Press, Inc.

Library of Congress Catalog Card Number: 89-91228

ISBN 0-449-14590-5

Manufactured in the United States of America

First Edition: September 1989

For my mother, Mary Aquina,
who has the Irish gift of fantasy.

Chapter 1

★ ★ ★ ★ ★ ★ ★ ★ ★ ★

"Ooooof!" Monica Wright let out a cry of frustration. Then she quickly glanced around to see if anyone had heard her.

The big Fairfield High gym was noisy and crowded with other gymnasts, and Monica saw a few of them look over at her. Fortunately, her coach hadn't noticed the error.

Monica was working on her uneven parallel bars routine for the big upcoming meet against Carlton High, and she should have been able to catch the bar on the down swing—but she hadn't. The past few days she had been feeling as clumsy as a brand-new gymnast. How could this nightmare be happening to her?

Casey Benson, one of her two best friends and also her spotter at the moment, looked amazed. "Hey, what's wrong, Monica? You've done this routine a thousand times before."

"I don't know," Monica sputtered, fighting to keep tears from her eyes as she started her dismount.

1

But something told her she was just at the beginning of a major slump. She landed ungracefully on the bright blue mat, although she stayed on her feet, and then raised her arms above her head for a professional finish.

Monica supposed that she *looked* the part of a competent gymnast, anyway, with her new lemon-yellow leotard and a tiny matching ribbon in her hair. But looking the part was not going to get her anywhere—especially not to the Olympics.

Monica had often been told she was one of the prettiest girls at Fairfield High. She was reed-slim due to a lucky metabolism as well as several years of ballet and gymnastics training. She wore her shoulder-length black hair in a clip at the back of her neck to keep it out of the way while she worked out. She usually had a big bright smile for everyone.

This afternoon, however, Monica was not smiling.

"We all have our bad days," Casey said, evidently sensing that Monica was near tears. "Anyway, the bars never were your favorite."

"That's not it," Monica said in a low voice. "I can *do* this stuff, it's just that we never have enough practice time."

Casey raised an eyebrow agreeably. "Well, that's the truth. When we're working out at the Flyaway Club we can take all the time we want."

Monica nodded. "Exactly."

Casey rubbed more chalk on the bars for her friend. "I feel like I could use an extra three hours a day on the beam alone," she complained.

Monica suspected that Casey was just saying that to make her feel better. Everybody knew that Casey

Benson was dynamite on the balance beam—in fact, it was Casey's specialty. The petite Casey practically exploded with energy during her routines, gliding with strong, sure moves down the narrow piece of wood like a cat balancing on top of a ledge.

"Of course, today of all days," Monica mumbled, "has to be a shorter workout time than usual."

"Can't be helped," Casey said with a shrug. "It's just one of those cases where the gym has to be cleared out early."

"Of all days," Monica repeated, staring up at the bars.

"Come on, Monica. Back on those bars until you get on track," Casey said. "Chalk up again."

Monica went over to the tray and dipped her hands in the powdery, dry white chalk. She quickly dusted off the excess so that she could get back to work before her time on the bars was over.

That's the biggest problem, Monica thought as she signaled to Casey that she was ready to begin. *There's just never enough time.*

The Fairfield High School gym was huge and in fact, was one of the largest in the Chicago suburban area. Still, there was a limited supply of gymnastics apparatus for the girls, so the whole team had to take turns.

Monica wondered how the others managed to do so well on the usual five hours of workout time. It seemed as though her friends were pulling steadily ahead of her. Casey was getting ready to go for Elite status in the spring and so was Jo Mallory, Monica's other best friend. Monica seemed stuck right where she was, and she knew that was no way to get to the Olympics in 1992!

Feeling dejected, Monica tried again on the high bar. But her upper body strength didn't seem to be there this afternoon. Her timing was off and she kept playing it safe, which was not the way to approach the bars. She went through the moves in absolute dismay at her clumsiness and then plunked down once more on the thick floor mat.

"It's no use!" she said. "I've lost it on the bars!"

Casey looked very worried. A frown cut across her little face and she pushed back her bouncy brown curls.

"Are you okay, Monica?" she asked in a whisper.

Monica didn't answer right away. She didn't know if she was okay or not. She had to get herself out of this slump! It was so self-defeating.

"Maybe I should go do my floor routine," Monica said. "If nothing else, that would cheer me up. I could at least remind myself that I'm good at *something*."

"Maybe," Casey said. "But you were probably right when you said you need more time on the bars. I think it's just a matter of getting extra practice hours."

Monica made a face. "Sure, but how do I get them? You know your father—I mean, the coach— doesn't allow anyone here after hours."

Casey's face reddened slightly. Monica knew that it still was a problem for Casey to accept her father as coach of the gymnastics team. "Bear" Benson was a good, fair coach, and he was well liked by all the girls on the team. But that didn't change the fact that he was Casey's dad. After some initial problems, he and Casey had managed to work things out—but it wasn't easy for either of them.

"Maybe if you try once more," Casey urged. "If you concentrate, I'm sure you can get the choppiness out of your routine."

"Choppiness?" Monica laughed bitterly. "That workout was worse than choppy!"

But Monica took a deep breath and made another attempt at the bars. This time things were a tiny bit better; she felt she had some control in her arms.

"There, you see?" Casey looked triumphant. "What did I say? All it takes is practice!"

Monica swung down and managed a smooth dismount—nothing great, but it was acceptable. She reached for her small white towel and dabbed at the perspiration on her forehead.

"Not bad that time," Monica said. "But we're not talking gold medal, Casey—not even bronze or copper!"

Casey rolled her eyes. "I told you, anyone can have a bad day."

"It's more than that." Monica felt certain that all she needed was a little more practice. "Listen, I'm going to talk to the coach. Maybe there's something we can work out."

The coach's whistle signaled the end of the day's practice. Bear Benson was standing by the gym bleachers, directing the clean-up of the equipment. Girls in leotards began bustling around, moving the blue mats onto trolleys and closing up the chalk trays.

"Remember, girls!" the coach called out. "One week from tomorrow is the big Carlton High meet. We've come a long way this season, but Carlton is a tough, competitive team, as you all know. It'll be close, but one more great win and we'll be going into the League championship undefeated."

Jill Ramsey and her friend Ginny Evans were the first ones to start humming the team's favorite song under their breath. Several others joined in until the song became clearly audible in the big gymnasium. Coach Benson sent a dark glare in their direction and silence fell immediately.

"Ladies," the coach went on, "we can't rest on our past laurels. We look to the future—and at Carlton High, the competition will be fierce."

Monica raised her hand abruptly before she had a chance to chicken out.

"Yes?"

"What if someone's in a slump, Coach?" she asked. "I mean, what if we feel the need for some extra workouts? Sometimes I think we're not getting enough time at these after-school sessions."

"Really?" Bear looked surprised. "Five hours a day isn't enough for you?"

Monica felt foolish with everyone looking at her, especially the senior girls, but she persisted. "Not always," she answered.

Bear rubbed his chin. "I'm sorry to hear you're having trouble, Monica. Do any of the rest of you feel that way?"

Several of the older girls on the team groaned. "No!" one girl said out loud. "We practice enough as it is! I never have time for my homework."

Jo Mallory raised her hand. "Even so, Coach, if Monica's in a slump, couldn't the gym be opened a couple of nights a week for her? We'd be willing to spot for her."

Coach Benson shook his head solemnly. "Jo, I'm surprised at you! You know the rules as well as I do. No one is allowed to use this equipment unless there's a coach or an official trainer present."

"But Dad," Casey blurted out. "Er, Coach, I mean. Couldn't *you* come in a few nights to help Monica out? Just from now until the Carlton meet?"

"I'm sorry, but no. I wish I could." Coach Benson shrugged. "This week I have faculty and Athletic Board meetings every single night. There's no way I could be here in the gym as well."

"Are you saying there's no way for someone to get extra help? That doesn't seem fair," Casey argued.

"Maybe it's not fair, but there is no way that the school can provide extra help right now," Bear answered. "Maybe Monica could spend a few evenings at the Flyaway Club."

Casey turned to Monica with a cheerful grin. "We'll call Chip!" Chip Martin was the coach who worked with Casey, Jo, and Monica when the school gymnastic season came to a close. He coached at the Flyaway Gym Club, the private club that had once been owned by Casey's father. The Flyaway was like a second home to the three friends.

Monica began to feel hopeful. She'd get professional coaching, after all, even if she had to pay for it. Her parents were more than generous, especially when it came to Monica's gymnastics. Sylvia Wright, her mother, was a successful real estate agent, and her father, Don Wright, was an insurance broker who did very well. Monica was not a "spoiled" only child, by any means, but she could rest assured that her parents would help her out in a crisis like this.

When the gymnastics equipment had been cleared from the floor, Casey, Jo, and Monica hurried to the locker room. Casey got a quarter out of her knapsack and handed it to Monica.

"Here. Call Chip right away," she ordered, and Monica went to the pay phone in the corner. She dialed the familiar number, heard the phone ringing at the Flyaway, and then was dismayed to get a recorded message.

"Hello, you have reached the Flyaway Gym Club. We are closed for renovations and will reopen in approximately two weeks. If you'd like to leave your name and phone number at the tone—"

Monica put down the phone receiver. Closed for two weeks! That wouldn't do her the least bit of good for the Carlton meet.

Back at her locker, she told Jo and Casey about the renovations.

"Chip, where are you when we *need* you?" Jo called out in a melodramatic, half-joking way. "Renovations! This is a disaster!"

Monica slumped down on the wooden bench near her locker. "I might as well face it. I'm going to be useless in the Carlton meet."

"No, you're not," Jo said firmly. The slender blonde shook her head, and her long ponytail did a flip-flop. "First of all, Ms. Monica Wright, get yourself out of this negative thinking just by—well, trying some positive thinking."

"What do you mean?"

"I mean, try to look at the doughnut and not at the hole, Monica," she instructed.

"Huh? What doughnut?" Monica asked.

"It's an old expression of my grandmother's, telling you to look at what you do have." Jo smiled. "You're a good, all-around gymnast. You've always done well, and you will again. You'll find a way to get some extra practice if you keep trying. You can find a way to do anything!"

This unexpected pep talk was typical of quiet Jo, who was often the philosopher of the three girls. Monica knew that Jo had vast experience in overcoming obstacles. She was one of six children, and the Mallorys never had enough time or money to go around.

Jo had tons of chores to do at home along with her schoolwork, but she always made extra time, somehow, to keep up with gymnastics. In fact, Jo was easily the most ambitious of the three friends; she was absolutely determined to become an Olympic champion.

So Jo allowed for absolutely no negative thinking whatsoever in her busy schedule. And, just realizing that, Monica felt ashamed of herself for letting such a little thing get to her.

"You're right." Monica squared her shoulders and gave Jo a thumbs-up sign. "I won't give in. I'll hang in there until I get my whole act together again."

"Atta girl!" Casey patted Monica on the back.

"We'll solve this thing together," Jo told her.

"I hope so," Monica whispered, opening her gym locker and pulling out her jeans and shirt.

Chapter 2

★ ★ ★ ★ ★ ★ ★ ★ ★ ★ ★

As Monica changed her clothes in the locker room, she tried not to think of her poor performance on the bars. All around her, her teammates were laughing, tossing around a stick of deodorant, exchanging gossip, and literally letting down their hair. But somehow the lighthearted atmosphere weighed even more heavily on Monica's troubled mind. To counteract her bad mood, she left the yellow ribbon in her hair and slipped into her brightly patterned blouse that looked great against her dark brown skin. Although it was one of her favorite shirts, it did little to cheer Monica.

"Monica, you look so sad," Jo commented. "I wish you wouldn't let this slump get you down."

"Thanks, Jo," Monica said.

"Oh, I know something that'll make you happy!" Casey jumped up with agility to balance on the locker room bench as if it were a beam. "You two are not going to believe this, but I've talked my parents into letting me have a slumber party next week!"

"That's great news, Casey," Jo said. "I thought your folks said never again after that awful sleep-over in fourth grade."

Monica chuckled as she recalled Coach Benson, at the time, groaning that the girls' party in his home had been worse than anything he'd ever lived through, including basic training for the Army.

"That one was pretty bad, wasn't it?" Casey grinned. She had a smile that could light up her whole face when she was really amused by something. "Ohhh, do you remember poor Hildy Cooper crying all night long?"

Monica smiled. "Hildy was so scared of that horror story someone told, about the girl who got stabbed and then was scratching on the outside door for help—"

"And no one would open the door because they thought it might be the murderer!" Jo interrupted.

"Jo, you're the one who told that story!" Casey pointed an accusing finger at her friend. "Good old Jo and her scary stories."

"A lot of the girls couldn't sleep at all after that," Monica added. "They were such babies!"

"And everyone got so-ooo overtired," Casey said. "But anyway, that's history!" She gave a the-atrical wave of her sturdy arms and turned like a circus performer. "We're in high school now, and we can have a civilized slumber party."

"Sounds terrific, Casey." Jo grinned. "And what's the occasion?"

Casey stuck out her tongue. "You know perfectly well. It's my birthday, of course."

"Really?" Jo said, pretending to be surprised. "Then I suppose you're going to expect us to bring birthday gifts, too?"

"Only if you want to be let in the door," Casey teased. "The whole gang will be there."

Monica tried to look enthusiastic, for Casey's sake. "And when is this great gala party?"

"Next Saturday night," Casey said, climbing down from the bench. "The day after the Carlton meet."

The Carlton meet. A feeling of dread seemed to invade Monica's heart when she heard those three words. She wished she could get more excited about Casey's party. She hated feeling like such a deadbeat. It was so unlike her.

But then, she thought as she stared into her locker mirror, sometimes a girl was entitled to her feelings—especially when her lifelong ambitions in gymnastics were at stake.

Monica had been working a long time to become a top-notch gymnast. When she was very young, she had studied ballet and had dreamed of becoming a ballerina one day. She'd been pretty good, too, for her age. But somewhere around fourth grade she'd become close friends with Casey, who had asked her to come along to try out the Flyaway Gym Club.

That first day at Flyaway, Monica had become convinced that gymnastics was much more fun than ballet—to her, anyway. It was tougher, she felt, because of the variety of apparatus a girl needed to conquer. And it was challenging in quite a different way from ballet. So she had joined the Flyaway Club as a regular, putting in long, grueling hours through the years.

Now, at age fourteen, Monica loved being part of the school team, and she loved working on her personal best with an eye toward the Olympics.

The problem was, her personal best wasn't at its best.

She closed her locker door dejectedly. Trying to find a solution was starting to give her a tension headache.

"You know what?" Monica suddenly said, turning to her two friends. "Instead of going home, I think I'll walk over to that brand-new gym. What's the name of it?"

Jo frowned, trying to remember. "I think it's called Northlake Gymnastics Club. I saw an ad for it when it opened last spring."

"Thanks," Monica said. "I might as well give it a try, right?"

"That's what I call real positive action. Want us to go with you?" Casey asked.

"Thanks, but no. I need some time by myself," Monica said. "I've got to do some thinking."

"You'll be okay, Monica. That extra time at the gym club will do the trick for you," Jo said in a low voice.

"Okay, I'm heading out then," Monica said. "The gym's not far from here. I'll talk to you guys later."

"Good luck!" Casey and Jo called out in unison. Casey added, "Call later and let us know what happens."

"I will." Monica slipped into her bright red parka and matching scarf, grabbed her shoulder purse and her tote bag, and left the locker room by the exit that led out to the school parking lot.

A cold wind was blowing from the direction of Lake Michigan, although the late afternoon skies were a vivid, cloudless blue. Usually it was after seven-thirty when workouts finished, and it was completely dark. Today, since practice had been shortened, Monica had the opportunity to see daylight for a change.

Fairfield High was in a great spot. The big, low, modern school sat on a slight hill so that it commanded a fairly good view of Fairfield. But that meant that whenever there was any wind, the school was one of the coldest places in town. Monica felt her scarf whipping around her neck like a flag atop a flagpole, and her fingers soon became numb as she walked along the path toward Main Street.

Still, in spite of the cold, the walk felt good. Sometimes Monica just needed to get away by herself and think. She knew she shouldn't have let today's failures bring her down so much. She should be happy that she was terrific at floor exercises.

I'm a dancer, Monica thought defensively. And that was why she was so at home on the floor routines. She just wished she didn't get uptight about her lack of uneven bars skills. It would all come back in time, it would. It had to!

She kicked at a pile of autumn leaves that had gathered near the sidewalk. The fallen leaves gleamed their reds, yellows, browns and rusts in the waning sunlight.

Before she knew it, Monica had reached the Northlake gym. She was impressed; the place looked like an extremely up-to-date facility. Feeling increasingly hopeful, she ducked inside. The heated interior felt nice after her chilly walk.

Monica found herself in an outer lobby, where a pair of double doors blocked any view of the gymnasium.

"Hi," Monica said to a young woman in a sleek red sweat suit.

"Hello, I'm Christy Mayes, the owner. May I help you?"

Monica stepped forward, introduced herself, and asked about available slots for immediate training.

"Gosh, I'm so sorry," the woman said. "We're totally booked at the moment. There won't be an opening for—I don't even know how long. It seems as though every little kid in town wants to learn gymnastics lately."

Monica nodded, feeling her hope start to fade. "But are you sure there's absolutely nothing? I just need some time on the bars for a week or so, just until an important meet. I can pay whatever your rates are—"

"I'm sorry," Christy Mayes repeated. "We really have nothing. We're overbooked as it is, and our staff is short at the moment. I just can't fit you in."

Monica sighed deeply. She felt almost rooted to the spot, as if by staying she could somehow convince the gym's owner to give her a little time.

A minute or so later, a boy who looked very familiar to Monica came sailing through the doors.

Monica had seen him before at school, she was sure of it. He was a great-looking black boy, not tall but sturdy, muscular, and powerful in build. She was almost positive that she had seen him on the boys' gymnastic team.

When he saw Monica, he stopped. "Hi," he said in a quiet, almost shy voice. He smiled tentatively, revealing straight white teeth. His dark brown eyes sparkled in the brightly lit entryway.

"Hi," Monica said in return.

"You're on the girls' gymnastic team at school," he said with quiet certainty. "You're the one who dances so beautifully on floor."

"Oh." Flustered for a moment, Monica simply stared back at him. "Thank you. How did you guess that I was in dire need of a compliment today?" she asked.

The boy threw his head back and laughed. "I didn't guess that," he said. "I was just being honest. I've seen you perform. You're incredible."

Monica was speechless. Who was this guy, anyway?

"My name is Derek Stone," he said. "And you're Monica Wright—right?" He grinned at his own silly choice of words. "Wright, right. I'll bet people do that all the time."

Monica giggled. "Only the goony ones," she joked.

"So . . . what are you doing here?" he asked. "Are you a member?"

"No," Monica said. "Are you?"

"Not me. I'm here to get my little brother, Teddy. He's a beginner," Derek told her.

"Good for him." Monica smiled. "Well, I wish I could say I've seen you perform, but I haven't . . . yet."

Derek shrugged. "No great loss. I'm not exactly God's gift to Fairfield High gymnastics."

"Somehow I don't believe that. You look really strong," Monica observed.

"You didn't say why you're here," Derek reminded her, changing the subject. "Just hiding indoors from the cold wind?"

"No. I thought I could get a little extra training for my bars routine. But they're all filled up. And our regular club, Flyaway, is closed for renovations. I can't believe my luck!"

Derek's brown eyes registered sympathy. They really were wonderful eyes for a boy. Nature had given him long, thick eyelashes that Monica or any of her friends would have killed for.

"Trying to get in shape for the Carlton meet next week?" he guessed. Monica nodded. "Well, I can't help out with that problem, but I can offer you a milk shake," Derek said.

"What?" Monica looked at him, puzzled.

"A milk shake. At the dairy bar across the street. They specialize in Double Chocolate Challengers! I'm about a half hour early to pick up my brother, so I just thought we could wind down from workout together. What do you say?"

Monica realized that he was actually a out—sort of on a date! He was offering h shake, at any rate, and the chance to s come better acquainted. "Make that a diet soda and you're on," she said, smiling.

Outside, the air felt warmer to Monica. The wind didn't seem quite so harsh on her face, but she decided it was all in her head because she was walking with a boy.

"So, tell me about your little brother, Teddy," Monica suggested as she and Derek made their way to the crosswalk at the busy intersection.

Late afternoon sun filtered through the trees, sending slender shadows onto the sidewalk. Monica felt an odd, quickened rush of blood through her veins just walking alongside Derek. She wasn't used to being with a boy. Although she was fourteen, she'd never done any dating, and she didn't even have many boys as friends. She'd always been too busy with her gymnastics and her ballet lessons.

"My little brother?" Derek pretended to think seriously as they waited for the light to change so they could cross the street. "Let's see. What can one say about Teddy? He's a whirlwind, a human dynamo, a bundle of energy—"

Monica laughed. "And that's the reason you enrolled him in gymnastics lessons! To get him out of the house!"

"Sure. And my parents think my being in gymnastics has been good for me, too. Actually, I think they're pretty proud of me."

"My parents love the fact that I'm a gymnast, too," Monica said. "I think that's one of the things that's so rewarding about working so hard—seeing r parents' pride."

Derek turned to look at Monica. "I agree," he said quietly. Then he shook off the serious tone and grinned. "Parents!" he kidded. "You can't live with 'em and you can't live without 'em!"

"I'll drink to that," Monica said.

The traffic light changed and Derek Stone took her hand. They crossed the street together, laughing like old friends.

Monica's heart felt much, much lighter and she began to think that her problems would work themselves out, eventually. Meeting Derek just had to be a good omen!

Chapter 3

* * * * * * * * * *

FAIRFIELD'S most popular dairy bar, the Creamery, was almost empty at that time of the afternoon. Monica and Derek headed for a booth in the back.

"Thanks for coming with me, Monica," Derek said as they slid into their seats.

"Thanks for asking me," she replied.

They sat sipping at their sodas, listening to songs someone was playing on the jukebox, and talking. They talked about school, gymnastics, and their families. It was odd, Monica thought, because they seemed to have so much in common.

For instance, even though Derek had a brother and Monica had no siblings, it turned out that both their parents were unusually strict, although fair.

"My father's *so* strict," Derek said with a twinkle in his eyes, "that his friends often tell him he ought to run a summer reform camp for wayward boys."

Monica laughed. "Sounds like it would be gruesome!"

"It would. He'd have all those delinquent boys

out on a chain gang, probably busting up giant rocks." Derek grinned. "Dad feels that hard work is the cure for any crime."

"So does my father," Monica said, her eyes lighting up. "When I get grounded, it's always grounded with kitchen duty, or laundry patrol. Or I get to clean out the attic for a week."

"Our fathers sound a lot alike," Derek said.

They gazed at each other in a moment of quiet companionship. The distance across the dairy bar table seemed to shrink to almost nothing as they looked into each other's eyes.

Monica felt for a second that she and Derek were almost touching each other. *Something* was touching, at any rate. Was this what they meant by two souls reaching out to each other? If so, it was a nice feeling: warm and friendly and trusting.

Confused, Monica let her eyes drop to the red formica table and she fiddled with her straw wrapper. "I wouldn't want my dad to be any different," she said.

"Me either," Derek said. "Dad's a great friend to have, in spite of his tough rules and standards."

"I know just what you mean! Somehow you know you're loved when you have strict parents," Monica said. "You know your folks care about you."

"Monica?" Derek said quietly. He looked very serious all of a sudden. "I have a silly confession to make."

"What's that?" Monica asked. "You want a milk shake after all?" she joked, trying to lighten the mood.

"I've been watching you all season long," he continued, ignoring her joke. "I sneak over to see your team workouts whenever I can. I've been sort of . . . mesmerized by your dance routines on floor."

Monica stared at Derek with her mouth slightly open. She had no idea how she should respond to such a compliment!

"I don't mean to embarrass you," Derek went on. "I just thought you might have heard it from your friends, that I was always there watching you. Anybody could see that I'm just blown away by your performance."

"Really?" Monica finally managed. "That's the nicest thing anyone's ever said to me."

Derek stammered a bit. "I hope you don't think I'm weird," he said. "I just think you're wonderful to watch. You're a terrific gymnast."

"Thank you." Monica gave Derek's hand a squeeze, since he seemed so nervous. "You don't seem weird to me. But I'm sure there are a lot more interesting and sophisticated girls around school to watch!"

He looked astounded. "Sophisticated? Who cares about that? I can't stand girls with three inches of mascara and arms full of noisy gold bracelets!"

Monica had to laugh at Derek's strange definition of "sophisticated." She had only meant that she felt sort of young for him. He'd said he was sixteen and a sophomore. She was merely a freshman and, by all rights, still should have been at Prescott Junior High if the town zoning hadn't been changed around. But when she thought about it, age had little to do with one's talent in gymnastics.

Monica decided to change the subject. It was very awkward, she realized, to have a boy shyly confess that he'd been watching her for several months. Usually it was just the opposite! She always developed crushes on boys, who she admired from afar, too shy to introduce herself.

"Tell me about your gymnastics," she asked. "What's your specialty? If I'd been watching you all this time, what would I have seen?"

Derek looked down at his empty glass. "Not much. I do have some upper body strength and I'm not bad at rings. But the Olympics committee people aren't exactly knocking down my door at this point."

Monica could understand how discouraged he felt. She knew from her own recent experience how difficult it was to try as hard as you could and have that perfect performance elude you.

Suddenly Derek looked at his watch and stood up. "Can you believe it? Time's up. I have to pick up Teddy now. We can walk you home, Monica. Where do you live?"

"Thank you, but no," Monica said. "I've got to get going. It's not far from here."

"Are you sure? I'd like to make sure you get home safe."

"I'll be fine, really." She rose and slipped into her parka. "Thank you for the soda, Derek. I had a great time."

"So did I." He was staring at her as if he was afraid to let her out of his sight. "Can we do something together another time?"

"Like what?"

"I don't know. A movie?" he suggested.

Monica felt her heart rate speed up. This whole

thing with Derek was moving along so quickly! She wasn't sure how she felt about it. "Maybe. I'll ask my parents," she told Derek.

"Okay." Derek reached out and fixed her scarf for her, his fingers briefly brushing against her cheek. In that instant she felt all tingly, with a warm feeling that seemed to go all the way to her toes. "I'll call you," he said. "Oh—and good luck," he said, almost as an afterthought. "With your uneven bars problem, I mean. I wish there was some way I could help."

"I do too." Monica sighed, remembering that afternoon's practice. "See you at school!" she called out as they walked out the door and headed in separate directions. She hurried toward home, her head bent low against the rushing wind.

It was only afterward, when she was almost to her street, that Monica thought about Derek. Did he have a slight crush on her? And if so, did she like that idea?

"So?" Casey asked on the telephone that night. "Any luck?"

"Oh, hi, Casey. I'm glad you called." Monica clasped her fingers tight around the telephone. In her bedroom she had an expensive green plastic phone that was transparent so that she could see the machinery working inside.

"How did it go?" Casey inquired.

"No luck with the Northlake gym," Monica said. "They're full." Monica stretched out on her king-size bed and stared at her walls. She'd done her room completely in black-and-white, except for several big, red floor pillows.

"All full? That seems impossible," Casey said.

"I know. I did everything but beg on my knees," Monica admitted. She was getting tired of thinking about that problem, and she wanted to tell Casey that she'd gone out with Derek Stone after her trip to Northlake. She knew Casey would be just as excited as she was about meeting the handsome sophomore gymnast.

As a rule, Monica reported every boy who even said "hello" to her in the school halls. But for some strange reason, this time was different. Monica didn't want to say anything to Casey just yet. She couldn't imagine why she was inclined to be secretive. Was it because she liked Derek more than the other boys she'd met before? Or because she was afraid he would never really call her? Maybe this afternoon had been a fluke and he didn't like her all that much.

"Listen," Monica asked, "how are the plans for the slumber party coming along?"

"Great! I talked to a bunch of people this afternoon, and I think everyone I've invited is planning to come."

"Wow!" Monica exclaimed. "What are we going to do? For entertainment, I mean?"

"I'm not sure yet, but we'll plan something great."

Monica had to smile at Casey's genuine enthusiasm. She wished she could feel that lighthearted, but the memory of her poor bars performance still haunted her.

"And my folks said we can have the whole downstairs of the house," Casey continued. "We can sleep all over the living room and family room."

"Sleep? Did you say *sleep*?" Monica teased.

Casey giggled. "I think we're just so much more mature now. I mean, it's possible we might catch a few zees before morning."

Monica heard her mother calling her from downstairs. "My mother's looking for me, Casey. I've got to hang up now. Your party plans sound terrific, though."

"Good. Keep thinking of things to do, okay?"

"I will," Monica promised. "Got to go now. Bye!" She hung up the phone and ran downstairs to the kitchen, where her parents were cleaning up after dinner.

"Hey, sport!" Mr. Wright said when Monica walked into the kitchen. "How about lending a hand?"

"Here I come." Monica grinned. "You know I'm always very eager to help." When both her parents groaned in protest, she continued, "No, really. This gives me a chance to talk to you guys about something. I didn't know if I should bring this up during dinner."

"Oh oh." Sylvia Wright pretended to be worried. "Sounds pretty terrible. Are they kicking you out of school?"

Monica laughed. "No, not that I know of!" She unfolded a soft, striped dish towel and began drying one of the copper bottom saucepans. "I just wondered what the rules are going to be . . ." She paused for a moment. "About boys. And, uh, dates."

There was silence for a moment or two. Then

Monica's father cleared his throat. "I guess we haven't really discussed this too much, have we?"

"It never came up before, Dad," Monica said.

"And now?" Mrs. Wright asked. "Has something come up?"

Monica shrugged and hung the pan up on the wall by the stove. "Maybe. I met this boy today, Derek Stone. He's a gymnast and goes to Fairfield High—"

"How old is he?" her father demanded, interrupting Monica.

"Sixteen. He seems really nice. We met after school today. He was picking up his little brother at the gym. He mentioned going to a movie or something, but when I told him I'd have to ask you first, he said fine." Monica knew she was babbling, but she had to convince her parents that Derek was responsible.

"Sixteen!" Mr. Wright repeated, looking stricken.

"That doesn't seem too old, but we'd definitely have to meet him, dear," her mother said gently.

"I wonder if he *drives*," her father growled, pacing around the floor with a deep frown on his face. "I don't like the idea of you going off with some new driver!"

Monica smiled. It was going to be a long discussion, she could tell. The interrogation was just beginning, and then the ground rules would be laid down. She took another pot out of the drainer and started drying it methodically. Yes, it would be a long evening. But as she'd said to Derek that afternoon, she wouldn't want her parents any other way.

Chapter 4

★★★★★★★★★

"GET those legs forward and upward! Bend sharper at the hips. That's it, swing back."

Jo was spotting for Monica the next afternoon. She was also doing a fair amount of coaching as Monica struggled once again on the uneven bars. Monica felt she was doing just as poorly as she had the day before, but she was grateful that Jo, who was an absolute wizard on the bars, was taking the time to offer her advice.

"You're a tough coach, Josie," Monica said, grunting as she did her swings.

"Straighten your legs!" Jo ordered. Her eyes narrowed as she concentrated on her friend's performance. "Listen to me. Straighten them, Monica."

"Okay, okay. How's this?"

"Better," Jo conceded.

It was a typical afternoon in the Fairfield gym. The noise level was fairly high, because in all sections of the enormous gym the equipment was in use by gymnasts at their workouts. The boys' team worked out in the other half of the gym.

Dozens of blue mats were spread almost wall to wall and they reflected the bright overhead lights.

"Time's almost up, you guys," Ginny Evans, a senior who wasn't noted for politeness or consideration, reminded them. She and her spotter were waiting for their turn on the bars.

"Already?" Monica asked. She dismounted in a hurry, putting no spirit or spring into the movement at all.

"That was awful," Jo told her. "There's no excuse for a sloppy dismount like that."

"But I felt so rushed," Monica complained. "I was just starting to improve with your coaching, and then—zap. It's time for the next person."

"I know, Monica, but you can't just give up like that." Jo looked seriously annoyed. "We all have practice problems at times."

Monica bent over and did one of her stretching exercises. When she raised her head, something made her look across the gym at the section underneath the basketball hoop. Her heart did a funny flip-flop. There was Derek Stone, just as he had told her, standing there on the sidelines, watching her.

Two bright spots of red colored Monica's cheeks, and Jo sensed her discomfort.

"What's the matter?" she asked, following Monica's gaze. "Who's that boy over there, anyway? I've seen him hanging around."

"He's a new friend—I think." Monica was still concerned about her bars routine, but she allowed herself to remember the moment when Derek had fussed with her scarf before they left the Creamery. The memory made her feel good. She saw Derek wave to her, and she waved back.

"Hello? Ground control to Monica," Ginny interrupted impatiently. "Are you two through here, or what?"

"It's all yours," Monica said graciously. It was odd how she felt sort of warm all over, almost as though she'd stepped outside on a wonderful sunny day. She'd always thought it would be neat to have a boyfriend, but she'd never imagined that it would affect her emotions quite so much.

She headed over to the other side of the gym to practice her floor routine. She wasn't sure whether she liked the fact that Derek would be watching her . . . or not.

When that afternoon's floor workout was over, Monica did have a little of her self-esteem back again. She had done very well on her floor exercise, so well in fact that she was bombarded with unexpected compliments from the other girls on the team—and from Bear.

"Wonderful, Monica," the coach said, clapping his hands together lightly.

With his gray curly hair and his intense dedication to gymnastics, "Bear" Benson would actually be scary looking, Monica often thought, if a person didn't know what a terrific, kind man he was. She'd known Coach Benson for a long time, and yet she still often thought that she wouldn't want to cross him in any way. He was a strict coach. He had his rules, and any team member who tried to get away with breaking them—even Casey, his daughter—was severely punished.

"Thanks, Coach." Monica smoothed a few wisps of hair back from her face. "I only wish I could do that well—or half that well!—on bars."

"Patience. You'll get there," Coach Benson told her gruffly. "You do realize, Monica, that there's nothing I can do about getting more practice hours for you."

"Yes, sir," Monica said in a low voice.

"There's just no time, not this week."

"I'm going to do terribly at the Carlton meet next week," Monica couldn't resist saying. "I just haven't got it together, Coach, not on the bars."

"I noticed that. If I could," he said gently, "I'd hire a whole bunch of new trainers and assistant coaches to help you at night." He held out his big hands helplessly. "But that's just not in my athletic budget."

"I know." Monica looked down at her feet and sighed.

"Sometimes these slumps disappear overnight," Bear said.

"Really?"

"Oh, sure. You'll be all right, Monica. Most likely this slump will pass in a few more days. You'll knock 'em all dead at Carlton, trust me," he told her.

"I wish I could believe that," she murmured.

"Then we've got Leagues, then with any luck the state championships. You've got plenty of time, Monica," Coach Benson assured her. "And of course, you'll be trying out for Elite in the spring, too."

"Right," Monica said listlessly. "If I get my act together by then!"

"You will. I'll see you tomorrow," Bear said. "Get a good night's sleep tonight. It will help," he urged in a fatherly tone.

Coach Benson wandered off to the boys' locker room and Monica looked around to see if Derek was still in the gym. When she didn't find him, she felt a strange sense of disappointment.

But when she started folding up one of the blue floor mats, there he was, right beside her, helping her with the other side of the mat.

"Hi," he said amiably.

"Hi." She smiled to hide the fact that butterflies were fluttering in her stomach.

"I saw your floor routine. It was *great*."

"Thanks, but I imagine you saw me on bars, too!" Monica commented.

"Yeah, well, that wasn't so perfect, but don't worry—you'll get it soon." He paused to fold his corner of the mat. "So, what did your parents say? Did you ask them if we could see a movie or anything?"

Together they finished folding the mat and stacked it on one of the piles.

"My parents said they'd have to meet you, naturally," Monica said.

"That's no problem." Derek's face lit up. "Do you think . . . could I drop by this evening?"

"This evening?" Derek's request took Monica by surprise. "I guess it would be all right."

"Oh. You probably have a lot of homework to do."

"I do, but . . . hey, Derek, are you any good at algebra?" Monica asked.

"Yes! It's my best subject," he bragged. "I can tutor you, if you need help with X's and Y's. Just don't ask me to help with English. I'm going crazy with my own class!"

"Are you?" Monica reached for another blue floor mat and started to fold it. "Well, I just happen to be an A student in English," she told him, grinning.

He stared at her for a moment. "Do you think your parents would let us try studying together?"

She shrugged. "I don't know. Probably."

"We could go to the public library for an hour or two," he suggested as he helped her with the mat. "We could do homework together."

"That sounds great," Monica said. "I've never been to the library at night."

"Oh, it's perfect there for studying. They even let you talk, if you need to." He grinned. "But believe me, I'm a hardworking guy when it comes to schoolwork."

"Are you? So am I."

"I'm bucking for every kind of scholarship there is, someday," Derek said. "I plan to get into some really great college, like MIT or Rensselaer or Cal Tech."

Monica was becoming more and more impressed by Derek Stone. "I'll ask my parents about going to the library tonight," she said. "How about eight o'clock?"

"You've got it."

Together they placed the next mat on top of the others that were piled up and went for the next one. They were pretty good at this teamwork stuff, Monica thought. Who knew what else they might be able to accomplish as a team?

"He *is* a nice boy, Monica," Mrs. Wright whispered.

It was later that evening and Derek was in the living room talking science projects with Mr. Wright. Monica's father was telling him how he had won First Prize in his high school's science fair years ago.

"I built a robot that astounded the judges," Mr. Wright said proudly.

"You must have been years ahead of your time," Derek complimented him.

"Yes, you could say that. My teachers wanted me to be a scientist," Mr. Wright said.

"Sounds like you should have been one."

In the kitchen, Monica smiled. Derek always managed to say the right things. And he was so polite that he was almost sure to convince two overly strict parents to let him take their only daughter on a date. At least Monica hoped that would happen!

In the end her parents decided they liked and trusted Derek. Monica was given permission to go to the library with him in the early evenings, provided they were going to do homework together. As far as movies and other dates were concerned, however, that remained to be seen.

But Monica didn't care—she felt overjoyed. She was going to be allowed to go out with a boy—a boy she liked!

She and Derek bundled up against the cold and walked the few blocks to the public library, a big stone building with turrets and round towers that looked a little like an old English castle. Thick green ivy climbed some of the stone walls, and at night, Monica noticed, there were patches of shadow behind the ivy.

Inside the library Monica and Derek set up their books at a round oak table in a room that was full of bookshelves, art exhibits, and lots and lots of books, of course.

They spent nearly an hour poring over Derek's outline for a paper on a short story that was due the next Monday.

"You need to write more about the plot," Monica told him. "For instance, what was the protagonist's goal? It doesn't seem clear to me, from your notes."

"The *who's* goal?" Derek looked befuddled, and Monica smiled. It made her feel important to help him, and he really needed the help when it came to English. She explained further about the protagonist, the main character of the story.

"In this particular case," she went on, "you have to mention that your hero undergoes a spiritual journey—from ignorance to the realization of his own true nature."

"Wow. That sounds heavy," Derek grumbled. He was eagerly writing all of it down in his notebook, however.

"You can make this a really great paper," Monica said. "All you have to do is give examples of his internal struggles."

"Sure." Derek laughed as if she'd said something hilarious. "It seems easy to do with *you* sitting here, Monica."

The way Derek was looking at her made Monica slightly uncomfortable. He seemed so impressed with her! But English was just one of those things that Monica took for granted, like being able to do a pirouette or an arabesque.

Before they knew it, the library was getting ready to close and they had to pack up their stuff. They put on their jackets and went back outdoors into the cold night.

"Wait," Derek said. "Let's take a walk around to the side. Do you like the gardens?"

"Sure," Monica answered. "But I have to get home pretty soon."

"Okay, we'll just check it out for a few minutes," Derek assured her.

They walked leisurely around the big fountain in the center of the library gardens. It had always been one of Monica's favorite places. Having formal gardens at the library seemed to her to be the ultimate in artistic blending. Books belonged with flowers, somehow—so much of the poetry she liked was about the beauty of nature.

Their footsteps clicked along the flagstone paths as they passed the dormant sections of the garden, where the earth had been turned over for the winter, and the tall shrubbery was now winter bare. It seemed to Monica like a magical spot.

And now, tonight, there was the added element of the dark evening and the many twinkling stars up overhead. Monica couldn't remember ever being beside the fountain at night before.

Monica wasn't surprised when Derek took her hand. It seemed natural for friends, even new friends to hold hands lightly while walking around such a romantic place.

"Thanks a million for helping me with that English," Derek said softly. "I'm sorry we didn't get to your algebra."

"Oh, that's okay. I'm not having too much trouble with that," Monica said.

"Well, I wish I could repay you in some way. You really saved my life, helping with that report."

Monica didn't answer for a moment. All evening a bizarre idea had been growing in her mind, but she didn't even want to put it into words.

She looked at Derek and wondered how he would react.

No, she couldn't even mention it.

Strangely enough, it was Derek who brought up the subject Monica had been avoiding all evening.

"I know you'd like some help with your bars routine," Derek said matter-of-factly. "But that's something I can't help you with! I wish I could, though."

"Yes," Monica said slowly. "So do I."

If only you knew what I was thinking, she thought to herself. Her plan was crazy—dangerous, even.

But for all her determination to put it out of her mind, the idea wouldn't go away.

Chapter 5

■ ★ ★ ★ ★ ★ ★ ★ ★ ★ ■

"READY or not—here we go!" Casey called out as she, Monica, and Jo jumped out of Mrs. Mallory's car. It was Friday night and the threesome had decided to go roller skating at World of Wheels, an old wooden building on the outskirts of town that had been around since the days when their parents were teenagers. The place had a friendly look to it, even though the exterior was slightly shabby.

"Hey, this is gonna be fun!" Casey said as the three girls poked their noses in the front door. "We haven't done this in a million years."

"And it's about time," Jo said with a straight face. "We probably need the exercise!" The other two laughed at that, because Jo had just been complaining that she was physically exhausted after a long week of workouts.

"Same old place," Monica commented as they walked in.

World of Wheels looked, sounded, and smelled just as it had years ago, when they were little kids and used to skate on Saturday afternoons. In those days, though, they always had someone's parents to watch over them.

When you entered the rink building, there was that first blast of incredible noise—the hundreds of skate wheels clanging around the wooden floor arena. And there was music, loud and brash and slightly behind the times. The smell of the rink was the same old one: a mixture of wood varnish and refreshment-stand food, like hot dogs, mustard, and that eternal fruity punch in a plastic, gurgling container.

Casey breathed in deeply. "Yep, things never change here. That's what's known as nostalgia, I guess."

"Well, I for one can't wait to get rolling," Monica said, barely able to contain her excitement. The music was making her heart beat a little faster and her toes were itching to start around the rink.

She had always found skating to be the perfect vacation from gymnastics. It was so wonderfully mindless just to coast around the big oval, Monica thought, with nothing more on your mind than avoiding the other skaters. You weren't in competition for anything. You weren't trying to best your last performance. You had no judges to watch over you and award you a number . . .

Monica looked around; the old place was funny-looking and nobody even changed the decorations. There were school pennants on the wall that looked like they'd been around since 1950, and a couple of old, framed black-and-white photographs of famous rock'n'roll stars who had appeared there at about the same time.

The girls went over to the skate rental booth and gave their shoe sizes to the girl in charge.

"Hmmm," Casey said, looking around. "I wonder if Brett is here tonight?"

"Now why do you ask that?" Jo demanded, sounding annoyed. "I thought this was going to be girls' night. No makeup, no fancy clothes, no looking around for guys . . ."

"Well, it *is* girls' night," Casey reassured her. "And we are here to relax, I promise you. But Brett is a good friend and I just wondered, that's all."

"Come on, you guys, get your skates on and stop arguing!" Monica ordered. She had already paid her rental fee and was slipping into her white skates. "Who cares about boys?" she asked. "We're not like some freshman girls who are always on the lookout for the male population."

Just then she felt a tap on her shoulder.

"Hi, Monica," said a deep, familiar voice. It was Derek! She couldn't believe he was there.

It was an awkward situation because she hadn't told Casey and Jo anything about Derek yet, not even about him coming to her house the night before or their library study date. She wasn't sure *why* she had kept it all a secret, but she had.

It probably had something to do with that bizarre idea she had, the one that involved Derek and the help she needed with her bars routine. Her plan was so sneaky that she didn't want Casey or Jo to suspect anything.

"Uh, hi," she stammered.

"I didn't know you were coming skating tonight," Derek said with a cute grin. He was wearing a blue-and-white striped rugby shirt and a pair of faded jeans. When he smiled, Derek seemed even more shy than she had remembered him.

Monica was torn. She loved seeing Derek again, but she didn't want Casey or Jo to get mad at her.

"Well, to be honest, Derek," she said, "we're sort of having an all-girls' night."

"Oh, I understand." Derek winked at her. "No guys allowed, huh?"

She rolled her eyes. "Not exactly. I mean, not entirely."

"Okay, I'll buzz off." He was so amiable Monica wanted to hug him, like a loveable teddy bear. "Maybe later we can dance to a couples only song?"

"Sure." Monica shrugged. "I mean, maybe."

When Derek went off with his friends, Monica was bombarded by questions.

"Who is he? What's going on?" Jo demanded.

"When did all this happen?" Casey asked.

"What kind of secrets have you been keeping from us???"

"Monica, you'd better tell all . . ."

Monica didn't know where to begin. "There isn't that much to tell," she said. "I happened to meet Derek the day we got out early and I went over to the Northlake gym. He was there because his little brother is starting gymnastics."

"*And . . .*" Jo said.

"Well, it's not such a big deal. Yesterday after workout he asked if he could come over to meet my parents—"

"Are you kidding?" Casey interrupted, her blue

eyes registering surprise. "He came to your house?"

Monica hesitated. Usually she shared everything with Casey and Jo, but this time she wanted to play down the whole situation. She didn't want them knowing how interested Derek seemed to be in her—and vice versa.

"So did your parents like him?" Jo asked.

"Well, yes. They let us go to the library together. We did some homework there, and then we came home," Monica explained, leaving out their romantic stroll around the fountain in the gardens. "That was it," she said. "He took me home and said good night at my front door with a handshake—and a 'thank you' for helping with his English homework." Monica finished the story and stood up on her roller skates.

"I can't believe you didn't tell us before," Jo said with a smile. "A date with a sophomore. That's not such small potatoes, Monica Wright."

"Oh, honestly, it wasn't a real date," Monica protested. "Come on, let's get out and skate." She headed out into the heavy traffic of the rink. The speakers were blasting an old Elvis Presley love song, and Monica couldn't help smiling. It *was* sort of special, she admitted to herself, to have a boy who was interested in you—especially an upperclass boy as good-looking as Derek Stone.

"You know what?" Jo said, catching up to her. "Let's make a pact! We won't talk about or even *think* about gymnastics this whole night."

Casey skated up on the other side of Monica and took her hand. "Agreed," Casey said.

"You've got it," Monica said, nodding. And for the

most part it worked. For at least an hour, as she glided along happily, Monica didn't think about the upcoming Carlton meet at all. Gymnastics seemed far away.

Except for that one idea that wouldn't leave Monica's brain. She tried everything to blot it out, even doing some fancy skating in the middle of the rink where the expert skaters went. But it was no use. The idea was taking root and growing as if it were a strong, persistent weed.

And the idea involved Derek. That's what made it even more exciting to her.

The music stopped and the three girls separated, taking a short breather near the side rail. When the announcer on the loudspeaker announced that the next song was "for couples only," Derek came skating around the rink toward Monica.

"Do you think your friends will let you skate with me?" he asked with a small, secretive smile. Monica wondered why he looked sort of triumphant, until she turned around and saw that Casey and Jo were also being asked to "dance," by a tall, blond sophomore boy and a red-haired freshman.

"I asked my friends to skate with your friends," Derek admitted. "That way, maybe Jo and Casey won't come after me with tar and feathers for ruining girls' night."

"Very resourceful," Monica said. She watched as Jo and Casey skated off with the boys. Great! Now she could be with Derek for a few minutes. They took each other's hands and went out to skate to a nice slow number. Monica loved the feeling of Derek's strong, warm hand holding hers. They skated along in rhythm, with as much precision as if they were old friends who had skated together forever.

Monica wondered just how friendly Derek did feel toward her. "Derek . . ." she began, and then stopped herself.

"What?"

"I have something to ask you, sort of a favor . . ." Monica felt her muscles tense with nervousness. "No, never mind."

"You can ask me," Derek said confidently.

"No," she said. "It's too weird."

"You can ask *anything*." Derek looked solemn, and suddenly he guided her over to the rink's side rail where they could stop skating and be alone. "Come on. I owe you a lot, Monica. You really helped me pull my English paper together."

Monica looked at his boyish, innocent face. Above them, the revolving strobe lights were whirling, throwing rainbow colors on Derek and all the skaters she saw go by behind him. The flashing of patterns and colors made it look like a party scene. Monica wished she could just relax and enjoy the skating, instead of worrying about the Carlton meet.

Finally she decided to come right out with it. All he could do was say no. She'd blurt out her plan all at once before she could change her mind.

"Okay. I told you it was crazy, and it is." Monica spoke quickly and in a low voice, hoping no one else was listening. "Remember when you said you wished you could help me with my uneven bars problem?"

"Sure." Derek looked puzzled, but eager to help, so Monica went on.

"I was thinking about trying to get into the school at night next week—into the gym. I was wondering if you could help me. I'd like to get some extra workout time on the uneven bars before the Carlton meet."

"Wow," he said in a low voice, as if the breath had been knocked out of him. "That *is* strange."

"It's against the rules, I know," she said quickly. "But I need practice time so badly and the coach can't give it to me."

"Wow," Derek repeated. "Breaking into the school . . . I don't know."

"You don't have to answer right now," Monica said. "Just think about it."

She watched Derek carefully for a moment. He didn't seem completely against the idea at least.

"It wouldn't be too hard," she pressed him. "We could pretend we were going to the library, like last night, and then—I don't know, we could find a way into the school somehow."

"You mean you'd *lie* to your parents?" Derek asked.

"It's not lying, exactly," Monica said. "They think we're going to the library—and we will, afterward."

"Come on, Monica, it's still not being honest with them," he pointed out.

"I know. Derek, I wouldn't mention this at all if I didn't feel so desperate! My bars routine is terrible, and I need to do well in the Carlton competition. You realize that Leagues are only two weeks away, don't you?"

"Yes. I understand Monica, but . . ." Derek didn't finish the sentence. He shook his head.

"We don't have to decide right now," Monica reminded him.

"You're right." Derek looked relieved. "Let's finish our dance and have a good time tonight. We can talk about this later."

"Great," Monica said. "But you'll let me know sometime fairly soon?"

He smiled warmly, the tension gone from his face. "I'll let you know," he promised.

They clasped hands again and went out to finish a romantic waltz. Monica smiled at Derek and they tried a few fancy steps in time with the music.

"Way to go!" Jo called out as she and her partner skated by. Casey waved when she passed by them.

Suddenly, everything seemed wonderful to Monica. She was skating with a really handsome guy who seemed to like her a lot. Her friends were with her, too—and they approved.

This was turning out to be a great night. Monica had a feeling of hope again . . . hope that Derek might say yes and then she'd be able to get out of her slump!

"He's adorable, Monica." Jo was munching on a piece of pizza later that evening in the dining room at Monica's house. Monica thought that it was unusual for Jo to speak with her mouth full, but evidently Jo was both starving and eager to talk about Derek.

"Chew your food and swallow before you speak," Casey scolded in a motherly, teasing tone. "But as a matter of fact, Monica, our friend the pizza monster is right. The boy is seriously gorgeous. I'm glad you finally introduced him to us."

"I didn't have much choice," Monica said. "There you were, skating with his friends."

"Who were also adorable, if you must know." Casey grinned and reached for her second piece of pizza.

"Agreed," Jo said. "So whatever happened to our all-girls' night?"

"I guess we're getting to that age where boys look pretty good to us," Casey said. "I know Brett sort of makes my heart stop every time I see him in art class."

"Still, I thought we decided years ago that we'd never have time for guys and dates and all that," Monica reminded them. "We figured that we'd have all we could do just preparing for the Olympics and keeping up with everyday life."

"That's right, we did decide that!" Casey said.

"You have a point there, Monica." Jo sipped her orange juice. "So does that little speech mean you're no longer going to see Derek Stone?"

Monica hesitated. She thought of the sneaky plan she'd proposed to Derek earlier that night, standing by the side of the rink under the whirling lights. She had actually asked him to help her sneak into the school!

"I don't know if I'll see him anymore," Monica said in a low voice. "Probably not. I have no time for dates."

Monica's mind raced in many different dir one of them being—What if Derek says *yes*? we really do sneak in and use the gym ille was exciting to think about. It might mean she could turn things around in just a couple of sessions. She could work on all her routines, and with Derek to spot for her and coach her, she'd have it made!

But you have to be careful, she warned herself. *You don't want anyone besides Derek to know anything. Not anyone, and especially your two best friends, who would try to talk you out of it!*

"My dad will be interested to hear about it," Casey said with a grin, and Monica started.

"Interested to hear *what*?" Monica asked.

"Glad to hear that you're so dedicated to gymnastics that you're giving up guys for a while." Casey winked to show she was teasing.

"Oh." Monica sighed with relief. "Sure. At least until after the 1992 Olympics, anyway."

All three of them resumed their attack on the pizza. They planned to watch a horror movie next, and then they'd all fall asleep in Monica's king-size bed. This was their "sleeping over" routine, the same one they'd been following for years.

"I can't wait to see the Killer Tomato movie," Jo said, folding up the empty pizza box.

"Me neither," Casey said. "I hope it's as good as that Vicious Celery one." When Jo looked puzzled, Casey laughed. "Ha ha. Gotcha! I'm just picking on you and your scary movies!"

Monica didn't say anything. She was busy going over the plan she'd outlined to Derek in her head. Maybe it was a gamble, but it would be a harmless one. She hoped that he would agree to it.

She needed that extra workout time!

Chapter 6

★★★★★★★★★★

MONICA thought about Derek all weekend, but he didn't call. She didn't dare call him. Finally, by Sunday night, she decided that she must have blown it completely.

He wasn't going to help her with her crazy scheme, that much was obvious. And not only that, she'd ruined their friendship!

He must have decided that under no circumstances would he take a chance on losing his place on the boys' gymnastics team—not for a silly freshman girl who couldn't face up to her failures. Monica could hardly blame him.

With a sigh she settled down to do her algebra homework on the kitchen table. Sometimes on Sunday nights she chose to work in the big, cheerful kitchen rather than upstairs at her bedroom desk. It had something to do with wanting to be near her folks, who were in the family room watching "Sixty Minutes." The big room upstairs seemed lonely every once in a while.

Monica had just started the problems in her workbook when she heard a light tap at the dining room window. Curious, she went to the kitchen and opened the back door.

"What the . . ." She tried to peer into the darkness of her backyard, but saw no one. She flipped on the outdoor light switch. "Who's out there?" she demanded nervously.

"Me. Derek." He stepped out from behind a forsythia bush and gave her a mock salute. He seemed to be standing awkwardly, as though he was holding a package under his coat.

"Derek! You almost gave me heart failure!"

"I'm sorry. I didn't mean to," he said. "I saw you in the window and thought if I tapped, you'd know it was me. I was taking a long walk . . . trying to think things out."

Monica could guess what he was trying to think out—how to tell Monica *no*, above all.

"It's okay, Derek." She shrugged her shoulders. "I understand. I know you can't jeopardize what you've worked for so long in gymnastics.

"Can I come in, Monica?" Derek came closer to the back door. "I have something to give you. And besides, it's really cold out here."

"Oh, I'm sorry! Of course." She smiled and opened the door a little more widely.

Her parents chose that moment to come out to the kitchen to see what was going on. They'd evidently heard voices and felt the cold draft coming from the open door.

"Derek, what a surprise." Mrs. Wright looked

puzzled but pleased. "I didn't know you were coming over tonight."

"I wasn't supposed to, ma'am." Derek stepped inside and took off his woolen cap. He smiled broadly at the Wrights. "I was out walking and just took a chance that maybe I could see Monica for a few minutes."

"I suppose so," Mr. Wright said. "But don't make a habit of dropping by, Derek. From now on, call first."

"I will, sir," Derek assured him. He flashed a grin at Monica as if to say, "I know all about strict parents—remember?"

"I brought something," Derek said, "that you all ought to take a look at before you decide if you want it." At that he opened his long overcoat to reveal what he'd been concealing. It was a kitten!

Monica let out a squeal of delight. Derek handed her the kitten, a tiny bundle of golden fluff, almost the color of butterscotch candy.

"Isn't he sweet?" her mother said immediately. "Is he up for adoption, Derek?"

"Yes. My little brother brought home two of them, and my folks said we could only keep one. So this guy is yours—if you want him."

The kitten purred. Monica couldn't believe she was holding something so small and precious. She had wanted a cat for a long time, but her parents had never liked the idea. However, within minutes all three Wrights were enchanted by the kitten, and it was decided that they'd keep him. Monica was thrilled.

"I'll call him Butterscotch," she promptly decided. "Thank you, Derek."

A few minutes later, Mr. and Mrs. Wright went back to their television show, and Monica and Derek were alone again. She fidgeted, wondering what Derek was going to say to her. She could hardly stand the suspense.

"I guess you're wondering if I'm going to help you," Derek began, almost in a whisper. He walked over to the kitchen window and looked out into the darkness of the Wrights' back garden for a moment.

"Monica, I'm not the world's greatest gymnast," he said at last. "Still, I'd hate to get kicked off the team. And that's what would happen if we were to try that plan of yours and get caught."

"I know." Her heart and her hopes sank. So his answer was no! Well, it was what she'd expected. "I understand, Derek."

"No, you don't," he protested. "I really think you're a *great* gymnast. You have it all, dance ability, style, incredible ambition."

"Thank you," Monica said shyly, embarrassed by his compliment.

He turned away from the window. "I told you how I've watched your floor routines, and I think you're a perfect ten."

"Derek, now you're exaggerating!" Monica told him.

"No. I really believe your Olympic dreams will come true." He spoke carefully and quietly so that her parents couldn't hear him. "But I can see that right now, you might need some extra help. Everybody needs a friend's help now and then. So I decided. I'll help you," Derek declared, looking right at her. "Let's give it a try tomorrow night. All I can say is, let's hope we don't get caught!"

Monica's hand flew to her mouth in excitement. She wished she could rush over to Derek and give him a big, grateful hug, as she would have done if it were Jo or Casey. But of course she couldn't hug Derek! Instead, she snuggled her face close to the kitten in her arms.

"I don't know how to thank you," she whispered.

He waved his hand in the air. "You don't have to. Just be the best gymnast you can be, that's all."

It was a touching moment. Monica tried to think what she was supposed to say or do next. Finally, for lack of anything better, she said, "Hey, would you like a cup of hot cocoa?"

"I thought you'd never ask," he said, taking off his jacket.

"What's the matter with you?" Casey demanded early Monday morning. She stared at Monica. "Do you have a personal vendetta against poor Kermit?"

"I just slipped with the knife, that's all." Monica had almost cut the frog's leg off, accidentally. She tried to laugh the whole thing off, but she wondered if her hand was trembling a bit too much to do a good dissection. She felt nervous and jittery inside, as if she were about to embark on a life of major crime. It had been happening to her all morning.

Then she'd shake her head and tell herself to stop being so *stupid*! She wasn't going to be hurting anybody. She would be helping the team in the long run.

"So why are you trying to massacre a dead frog?" Casey asked again. "You don't seem to like yourself today, Monica."

"I'm fine. Really." Monica lifted another dissection instrument out of its case and tried to put the frog's leg muscles back into their correct order. "Yuck, this is a disgusting course!" she said to Casey. Even the strong smells in the science room were getting to Monica. She'd be glad when today's biology lab was over.

But American history, which came next, was no better.

"Monica Wright, you seem to be daydreaming," Mr. Dodge, her history teacher, complained.

"Oh, no," Monica piped up, embarrassed at being caught with her mind elsewhere. "I was right with you."

"And where *were* we, Monica?" Mr. Dodge inquired.

"At ... uh ... the Boston Tea Party?" Monica guessed.

Several kids in the class laughed, and Monica knew she'd guessed wrong.

Mr. Dodge was suppressing a smile himself. "No, we weren't at the Boston Tea Party. But as long as *you* were, why don't you tell us all about it?"

Monica hadn't read her textbook last night. She'd been too keyed up after Derek left, worrying about how they'd manage their break-in tonight.

"Um, the Boston Tea Party," she began. "It wasn't really a party, of course, it was an act of rebellion." She hoped she sounded self-confident and informed. "The colonists, uh, they didn't feel like paying taxes to England any longer, so they rebelled."

The word "rebellion" echoed in Monica's head after she had spoken it aloud. Wasn't that what she and Derek were planning to do—be rebels? They were disobeying the coach's direct orders—or she was, at least. Derek was only doing it because she'd asked him to help.

"Monica, that was very good," the teacher said, still smiling with amusement. "And now I believe we'll return to the real subject at hand—the drafting of the Constitution."

"The Tea Party was over long ago," Jo whispered from the seat behind Monica. "It's *history*, you might say!"

"Very funny," Monica muttered. She vowed to concentrate in her classes from now on—it did no good to worry about the future and wonder whether she could pull off her scheme.

She willed her hands to stop shaking. An athlete had to have complete control over her body. With those jittery fingers, she wouldn't even be able to complete a handstand!

At lunchtime, Casey and Jo slipped through the cafeteria line before Monica. They hurried over to their usual table and sat down, setting their book bags on a chair to save a seat for Monica.

"Before Monica gets here," Casey said, "I want to ask you something."

"I think I know what you're going to say," Jo interrupted. "Have I noticed something strange about her? And the answer is yes."

Casey sat back in her cafeteria chair, ignoring the food on her tray. It was a tuna salad sandwich, anyway, not her favorite lunch at Fairfield High. Her brother Tom had a saying about the school's tuna sandwiches—he always claimed the cafeteria staff made a fish swim through mayonnaise for a minute, and they called that tuna salad. After a few months at the school, Casey had to agree.

"What do you think it is?" asked Casey. "Did you see her over the weekend?"

"No. I was home the whole weekend, slaving away. You know what it's like when Mrs. Clean goes on a rampage."

Casey smiled. "You mean your mother? Actually, my mother was that way on Saturday, too. And Sunday we all went to visit my grandparents, so I never saw Monica either. I wonder if something happened?"

"She sure is spacey." Jo took a bite of her sandwich. Her philosophy was that an athlete in training always needed nourishment, no matter how bad the food tasted.

"She was actually trembling in science," Casey observed. "I think we ought to keep an eye on her, try to figure out what's happening."

"Sure." Jo shrugged amiably as she opened her milk carton. "I'm willing to play P.E."

"P.E. ? What's that?"

"Private eye," Jo said. "Don't you ever watch television? A detective is called a private eye—it comes from private investigator." Suddenly Jo looked embarrassed. "Oh, maybe I mean a P.I."

"Maybe you do!" Casey shook her head. "What a weird pair of friends I have," she said. "Quiet now. Here comes our suspect."

Jo turned to look. *"Clue number one,"* she said in a serious tone. "The girl is getting a hot lunch. Now why would any sane human being subject herself to such an ordeal—mystery meat and lumpy potatoes?"

"Ugh. Scary, isn't it?" Casey asked. "There's definitely something going on in the secret life of Monica Wright!"

Jo nodded. "And we'll find out what it is, one way or another."

"One way or another," Casey repeated with a wink.

Chapter 7

★ ★ ★ ★ ★ ★ ★ ★ ★ ★

THE sky had been dark and overcast the whole afternoon, and now there was a damp chill in the Illinois night air. It looked like snow would start falling at any minute.

Now that the time had come for the break in to the school, she didn't even feel nervous. She told herself she was doing the right thing. *No guts, no glory*, she thought.

Monica and Derek walked cautiously along the long, winding driveway that led up to Fairfield High School. All was quiet that night, with no cars coming along either to or from the school.

"Skulking around like this really feels weird," Monica whispered as they cut across a worn, short-cut path that had been used by thousands of students through the years. The path led through a stand of evergreens and black birches, and in the daytime birds chirped noisily at the kids who cut through there. Now, in the dark, the only sound that could be heard was the crunch of Monica and Derek's footsteps across the frozen grass.

"Doesn't it feel strange, being here at night?" Monica asked.

She thought Derek grunted in agreement, but she couldn't be sure. He'd been oddly silent ever since they set out from Monica's house, books in their arms, looking very much as if the library was their destination. Mr. and Mrs. Wright had both smiled and told them to study hard.

"Be sure you don't get home late, Monica!" Mrs. Wright called out.

"Don't worry," Monica answered from the front steps. "I'll be back before ten."

At the time Monica thought that Derek's face looked pinched, somehow, and she knew it was because he hated the deceit.

"I hate sneaking around too, you know," Monica said as they continued their trek up the hill to the school.

"I know you do," Derek answered. "But I suppose it will be worth it if it helps you with the Carlton meet. Watch out for that branch!"

Monica stepped back. "Thanks."

"And anyway, we *won't* get caught," Derek said firmly.

How could he possibly feel so confident when they had no idea what they'd find once they got inside the dark high school? Monica wondered.

But when they reached the school, it was so brightly lit that it looked like Parents Night!

Monica gasped. "Who's here, do you think?" she asked Derek.

He didn't answer for a moment; he seemed to be checking out every corner of the building before them. "I think it's only the night custodians," he finally said. "There are only two cars in the parking lot, see?"

"Yes. Do you think we should still go on?"

"We can try. Let's circle around until we find a wing that's good and dark."

They walked around the building quietly, peering into lighted classrooms. The custodians seemed to be cleaning both in the south wing and in the east. But when Monica and Derek reached the north wing, they found it was dark.

"Aha!" Derek whispered triumphantly. "I'll bet they've already cleaned this section. Per-fect-o!" He jumped up on the window ledge and pried at the window.

"It's locked, isn't it?" Monica asked nervously.

"No, I don't think so . . . it's just stuck . . ." At that moment the window slid up half an inch. "All right, we're in business," Derek said cheerfully. He pushed harder, but couldn't seem to make the window budge any farther. He looked as though he was losing his patience.

"I can help, too, you know." Monica leapt up onto the ledge beside him.

Together they made the window slide up about two feet—plenty of room for two slender gymnasts. They squeezed through and dropped silently to the floor.

"Where are we?" Monica asked.

"Looks like Mr. Olsen's English room to me. Watch out, it's really dark here," Derek cautioned.

They had to feel their way around the desks one by one, finally finding the door to the hallway. Now came the really tricky part. They had to travel along two long halls until they reached the gymnasium.

"I can't believe we're doing this," Monica muttered. She could feel her heart beating more and more rapidly.

"Sshhh," Derek warned her.

Derek peered out into the hallway, then turned to Monica. "Are you sure you want to go through with this?" he asked quietly.

Monica didn't breathe for a moment. She was tempted to blurt out, "Let's get out of here while we can!"

But she didn't. They had come this far and there was no point in turning back until they'd achieved what they'd set out to—the extra workout time that would get her out of her slump.

"I say we go for it," she told Derek.

"Okay," Derek said. He sounded sort of grim, but didn't ask any more questions. They cautiously made their way out into the hall. Monica had half expected to hear a burglar alarm go off, but Fairfield High, at least this part of the north wing, was eerily silent.

As she tiptoed down the hall, Monica looked around incredulously. It was so quiet! There was no slamming of locker doors. No big football players lumbering around. Nobody in varsity jackets, nobody with spiked hair, nobody in faded denims, no hall monitors . . . this was absolutely unreal!

Monica stole a quick look at Derek. He must

have sensed the strangeness, too, but he seemed to be concentrating on the task at hand, which would be the safest way to get from point A to point B. He had said he was good at algebra; maybe he was a geometry whiz as well, she joked to herself.

They passed classroom after classroom, not stopping until they reached the first corner. There they hesitated and flattened themselves against the row of blue lockers. The smell of cleanser and floor wax was strong here, so they peered carefully around the corner. A dim light burned in the hallway beyond double swinging doors.

"Nobody in sight," Monica whispered.

"No, but I think the janitors are around somewhere," Derek said. He stayed close to the lockers.

Monica thought Derek looked very much the part of a cat burglar. He was wearing a dark turtleneck sweater beneath his navy pea jacket, making it possible for him to blend into the school shadows, if need be. Monica hadn't been quite that smart; she was wearing her usual red parka and a beige sweater.

"We can't stand here all night," Monica urged him, anxious to get moving again.

"Right. Let's go."

They crept onward, even more quietly than before. Now they were out of the classroom area and going past some of the faculty offices. Just the thought of the principal's office gave Monica a cold shiver all the way down her spine. What horrible punishment would they get if they were caught like this?

She willed herself not to think about it, just as she always tried not to even imagine falling off the balance beam. Some things you just had to plunge ahead and do no matter what.

Suddenly Derek grabbed Monica's arm and gestured toward the principal's office.

"That you, Dan?" called out a man's deep voice, about three feet away from them. A custodian was just on the other side of that door!

Monica and Derek scooted across the space of the doorway. But the voice called out again, impatiently, "Did you bring the mops? Is that you, Dan?"

"Yeah, it's me," Derek answered. Then he and Monica made a run for it. They sprinted down the hall and zoomed around the next corner, not even stopping to wonder whether Dan might be lurking somewhere. They had to get far away from that guy in the principal's office!

They practically flew along the short corridor to the gym. Fortunately, the gym doors were unlocked and they slipped inside.

Breathless, Monica stood still and looked around. The huge gym seemed even bigger than usual. The vaulted ceilings were dark and shadowy, and it was filled with silence as though a giant hand had reached in and turned off the volume button of Fairfield High.

Monica shivered involuntarily and looked over to see if Derek was affected the same way. But he still looked serious, and didn't appear to be enjoying this adventure at all. She knew she shouldn't have dragged Derek into something like this! It was immoral, illegal . . . and could even be dangerous.

"Well, we're here," Derek said softly. "I think it's safe. The custodians have already cleaned here, I can tell by the smell of the pine cleanser."

"Are you all right?" Monica asked, worried that Derek might be having second thoughts.

"I'm fine," Derek said in a clipped voice. "Let's get you started." Together they dragged out the equipment they needed—the bars, the mats, and the chalk tray. Monica stepped out of her street clothes and folded them neatly; she had worn her old workout leotard underneath. She started to put on her wrist guard.

"Wait." Derek looked at her and frowned with disapproval. "Aren't you forgetting something, like your warm-ups?"

"Oh, but"—She had almost said that they didn't have a whole lot of time to waste. But she could see from his face that he meant what he said—and of course he was right. No athlete could start without the correct warm-ups.

She plodded through her stretches while Derek adjusted the bars. For light, they had to be satisfied with the one small bulb that burned over near the basketball hoop. It was enough.

Every tiny sound echoed in the huge, empty gym. Monica completed her sit-ups, and then she was ready for her workout.

Derek was well qualified to be her spotter and her coach. He spoke in a low, quiet voice, advising caution and safety above all.

"I don't want to be *too* safe in my routine," Monica told him, feeling frustrated. "That's what got me in trouble in the first place!"

"You don't want to get hurt, Monica." His dark eyes blazed with emotion. "Nothing is worth that."

"Okay, okay. Lighten up, coach." Monica grinned and vaulted up to the low bar to begin her preliminary swings. Somehow she felt freer tonight, stronger, more in control.

In the all-too-quiet gym, every little sound was magnified. Even the small squeak of Monica's chalked hands could be heard as she rotated on the bars. Monica felt a rush of excitement as she went through her tone. She felt like the archetypal athlete working late into the night to polish her performance while the rest of the world was resting comfortably at home, watching TV and sleeping.

"Good, Monica, good," Derek called out softly.

She concentrated even more on her routine and gave it her all. Each time it got a little better, and Monica felt her confidence returning with each successful dismount.

She was soaring, agile, and full of grace. She was a highly competent gymnast who had taken charge of her life—and her sport. It was exhilarating. When the practice session was over, Monica couldn't help smiling in triumph.

"That was great," Derek said. "Almost every minute of it."

"I shouldn't say it, but I think so, too." She mopped her forehead with a towel. "I can't imagine how to thank you, Derek."

"You don't have to," he muttered as he started to put away the apparatus.

"You've saved my career," Monica went on in a hushed voice. "And not just my high school team career. I mean my Olympic hopes! I can face the world again, after this."

"You can even face those girls from Carlton, can't you?" Derek asked with a grin.

"Yes, thanks to you."

"We're coming back tomorrow night, though," Derek said. "You still have to refine those handstands."

"I need more flexibility, don't I?" Monica asked, although she felt relatively unconcerned about it. She'd get it right; all it would take was another good, long workout session.

"*Lots* more flexibility." Derek spoke gently but firmly as he started putting away the equipment they'd used.

"Okay, coach," Monica answered, giving him a mock salute. She slipped into her clothes quickly, then pitched in and helped to move the bars. When she and Derek left the gym, there was absolutely no sign that anyone had been in there, much less used the equipment. No one could possibly guess about their little nighttime adventure.

Getting out of the school seemed much less hazardous than getting in. The custodians were nowhere in sight, and when Derek and Monica got outside, they saw that the parking lot was completely empty.

"So, now we know their working schedule and when they leave," Derek observed.

"At least we hope so."

"Right. We hope so."

Snow had begun falling lightly but steadily. The grounds of Fairfield High reminded Monica of a Christmas card, with fluffy snowflakes clinging to the evergreens and oaks.

"Should we be worried about our footprints?" Monica asked as they moved quickly toward the shortcut path.

"I don't think so. Not tonight," Derek said. "If it keeps snowing for a few more hours, our tracks will be well covered."

Monica breathed in the cold, bracing air. "Even Mother Nature is conspiring to help us."

"Mm-hm," Derek mumbled. He didn't sound convinced. Monica decided that he must be more of a realist than she was. Well, after all, he was going to make science or engineering his career. He needed to think logically. But Monica was more of a dreamer. First she had wanted to be a ballerina, and now she dreamed of being an Olympic gymnast.

That thought made her feel glad, all over again, that they had pulled off this break-in stunt. It would help make her dream come true in the long run.

She smiled as a snowflake lightly touched her face.

She was on her way.

Chapter 8

* * * * * * * * * *

"WAIT till you hear this!" Jo stopped Casey just before she went into art class on Tuesday.

"Hear what?" Casey asked.

"I checked up on Monica last night." Jo had a smug expression on her face that said I-told-you-something-was-up.

"And? What did you learn?"

"I called her house," Jo said. "She wasn't home." Casey shrugged. "So?"

"Her mother told me she went to the library again—with Derek Stone!" Jo announced.

Casey grinned. "That doesn't exactly sound like a major crime to me."

"Casey, don't you get it? She's seeing a lot of this Derek person. Much more than she's telling *us* about."

"And we're supposed to be her best friends!" Casey complained.

"There's more." Jo paused for dramatic effect.

68

"Her mother told me that Derek brought Monica a kitten! And the family decided to adopt it."

"What? Why would she keep a *kitten* a secret from us?" Casey asked, obviously amazed that Monica, who was always so talkative, hadn't shared this with her friends. "Monica never said a word about any kitten," Casey repeated indignantly.

"I know. She's really been hiding something from us. And now we know what it is . . . part of it, anyway."

"We do?" Casey looked puzzled. "What do we know?"

"Well . . . we know that Monica must like this guy Derek more than she's admitting."

"This is so unlike her," Casey said. "Do you think we should ask her about the kitten—and these library dates?"

"Not yet. I have another idea," Jo said. Just then the bell rang, beckoning everyone to class. "Oh, great. Now I'll probably get a detention."

"Hey, that's okay," Casey said with a grin. "After all, you're the world's cleverest P.E."

Jo shot her a look that could kill. "P.I.," she corrected. "We'll talk later!" she called out as she dashed off down the hall.

Monica sailed through her classes on Tuesday morning just as she had sailed through the air the night before. Her hands didn't tremble at all that day. There was just one small thing, but she didn't think it was significant: her stomach kept gnawing in a funny, painful sort of way.

Just before lunch, Monica stared into her hall

locker trying to remember which books she needed
for the afternoon. She thought about the progress
she'd made the night before on bars. She and
Derek weren't going to get caught! They had the
system down pat now.

She smiled as she saw Derek walking toward
her. It was the first time she'd seen him all day. He
looked so handsome that her heart seemed to stop
for a second.

"Hi," he said. "How are you doing?"

"I feel great," Monica said cheerfully. "How
about you?"

He didn't answer right away. He appeared to be
looking at the magazine photos she had taped inside her locker. There were pictures of Mary Lou
Retton, Nadia Comeneci, the ballet star Mikhail Ba-
ryshnikov—and one wacky picture of Eddie Mur-
phy, just for fun. "It's hard to figure you out,
Monica," he finally said.

"What's that supposed to mean?" Monica stared
at him blankly.

"Oh, just that it's not easy for me to see where
you're coming from," he commented.

Monica shut her locker. "Nothing mysterious
about me," she insisted.

"Yeah? Well, how about that Watergate caper?"
Derek asked.

"Watergate?"

"That's what I call it." Derek grinned. "The
break-in. It's supposed to be a joke."

Monica smiled, but she didn't think it was very
funny. She was glad she had gotten the extra practice time, but she wasn't proud of the way she'd

done it. She decided to change the subject. "Aren't you going to ask about Butterscotch?"

"Sure. How is he?"

"Great! I love him. Mom says he has to sleep in the kitchen, in his bed, but twice now he sneaked upstairs and slept on my bed." She grinned happily. "He keeps my feet warm."

Derek nodded. "That's nice." Monica thought he looked distracted, as if he wasn't really listening to her.

"I'm so glad you brought us that little kitten," she added.

"I'm glad, too." He looked down at his feet.

"Are we still on for tonight?" she asked.

Derek shrugged. "If you want."

"Of course, I do." She patted him on the arm affectionately. "I have to meet Casey and Jo for lunch. I'll see you later."

After he'd gone off down the hall, Monica wondered what was bothering Derek so much. Now he seemed sort of sad, even disappointed. She had thought that their nighttime adventures would bring her and Derek closer, somehow. But so far it didn't seem to be working out that way.

Was he disappointed in her? Or was he just nervous about what they were doing?

Well, she couldn't worry about it. This would probably be the last night they'd break into the school, anyway. Tonight she'd work on her back aerial somersaults on the balance beam, and that would get her ready for Friday's meet. Then they could go back to their *real* library dates.

* * *

"I brought a flashlight tonight," Derek whispered as he and Monica approached the school that evening.

Another light snow had fallen that afternoon, dusting the whole town of Fairfield with a powdery white coat. They knew that now they'd be leaving footprints wherever they traipsed outdoors, but it couldn't be helped. They'd just have to hope that no one would have reason to notice two sets of footprints among the many around the high school. They'd have to be doubly careful inside the school, too, not to track wet snow all over the halls.

Derek held out his flashlight. It had his initials, D.S., etched on its stem. "I was a Boy Scout," he said. 'Always be prepared,' that's what they taught us."

They entered through the same window and found the room just as dark and deserted as it had been the night before. The rest of the trip, across the many hallways and past the principal's office, went much smoother, however.

"Where's that guy Dan and his buddies?" Monica asked as they looked around for the custodians. There was no sign of them anywhere.

"I don't know." Derek sounded worried. "I'd feel better if we could figure out where they are tonight, so we could stay away from them."

The gym was unlocked and as empty and silent as before. Efficiently, Monica and Derek set up the mats and apparatus. They had agreed beforehand that she'd work out on the balance beam this time, so they moved it to the center of the gym. Derek set up his flashlight so it would shine a bit more light on Monica. He went around checking everything while Monica did her warm-ups.

"Why not do your famous cartwheel?" Derek suggested. "I love seeing you do it on floor."

"I'm not so terrific on the beam," Monica warned him, but she grinned and hopped onto the beam.

For half an hour she worked on the basics, trying to strengthen the weak points and overcome her fears. Not long ago, in a practice, she had fallen from the beam, and that made her be overly cautious now.

"Come on, loosen up," Derek said once. "You don't have to take wild chances, but you do have to be more flexible. You know what I mean?"

"Yes," Monica answered, taking a deep breath. This was so wonderful, she was thinking. Not having to share the apparatus with anyone. No one waiting to take a turn, no one bugging you to get finished—

She decided to try a back aerial somersault, which was something new for her. Casey could do it with ease, and so could Jo, but Monica was still struggling to master it.

"Watch this!" she called out to Derek. "I'm going to do a back!" She glanced behind her at the beam, then turned back around to begin the move. She was sure she could do it!

"Wait a minute!" Derek warned her. "It's too dark to—"

But it was too late. As Monica jumped backward through the air, she made one little slip—with her right foot when she left the beam—one half of an inch of a slip—just enough to throw her off course.

She groped in the air, knowing she couldn't land on the beam.

"Help me!" she called out before she could stop herself. Her voice carried, loud and clear, and echoed through the cavernous gymnasium.

Derek wasn't able to catch Monica, and she crashed loudly onto the mat. Shooting pains traveled upward from her hand all the way to her elbow.

Derek rushed over to her. "Are you okay?" he asked.

"It only hurts when I laugh," she tried to joke. "And this wrist isn't exactly in the best of shape." Monica's eyes quickly filled with tears.

"There's no time to waste," Derek whispered. "That fall really made a huge noise, Monica."

"You mean?" She sat up, frowning. "You think someone heard us?"

"It's possible." Derek helped her stand up. "Grab your coat and stuff and let's go hide, just in case—"

He had no sooner spoken the words when they heard footsteps coming their way. It was the custodians!

"Let's go," Derek urged. "We can make it if you're not too hurt."

She *was* hurt, but luckily not in her feet or legs. Monica yanked on her clothes in record time and took off with Derek at a fast pace. They could hear the footsteps getting louder and nearer. Monica felt her heart racing in a way it never had before.

They had to get away! If they were caught now

it would mean getting thrown off the team for both of them!

They scooted out the side exit into an empty hallway just in the nick of time. Men's voices could be heard, loud and indignant, from somewhere near the beam.

"Somebody was here!" one deep voice called out with anger. "Look at this equipment!"

Monica and Derek exchanged a nervous glance. They hadn't had time to put away the things they'd used—and that could mean big trouble for everyone on the gymnastics team.

"Let's find them!" yelled another voice. "They couldn't have gone far!"

Derek and Monica started running, and didn't stop for a second. They sprinted down the halls until they reached Mr. Olsen's classroom, and then jumped out the window without even taking the time to close it after them.

Chapter 9

★★★★★★★★★★★

DEREK and Monica ducked into the library where it was warm and seemed wonderfully safe. They stayed in the outer lobby by the double doors and stood next to the old-fashioned radiator that was hissing steam and warmth.

"What a close call. I can't believe that just happened," Monica said, somewhat out of breath from the running.

"I can't either." Derek looked around to make sure they were alone before he spoke. "Monica, I think we'd better not be seen together tonight."

"But why? What—?"

"I have a problem," he said, "and I don't want it to become your problem as well."

"Are you talking about the footprints in the snow?" Monica asked.

"No."

They were silent for a moment as an elderly lady entered the lobby. "What are you talking about?" Monica demanded when the woman had gone past them. She felt like she was falling apart. Her wrist was killing her, and she could scarcely breathe after all that tension.

Derek didn't answer right away. "Do you remember my flashlight?" he finally said. "The one with the initials on it?"

She gasped in horror. "We left that there?"

Derek nodded. "I put it down when I helped you. Anyway, it doesn't matter right now. We've got to split up, Monica, in case anyone we know comes along . . ." Derek looked at his wristwatch. "I hate to do this, but can you get home by yourself?"

She blinked. "Of course. But I'm worried about you."

"Forget it. I've got to leave you, believe me." He was looking out the glass part of the library door, and all of a sudden his face constricted with worry. "I'll go out another exit," he said. "Here come your two friends."

"What?" Before she could utter another word, Monica saw that Derek had disappeared down the stairs that led to the library's basement. She hurried over to look out the top window pane of the front door. Sure enough, there were Casey and Jo, coming up the library's front steps!

Fortunately, they were caught up in their conversation and didn't see her.

Monica couldn't imagine why Casey and Jo were coming to the library, but for now the only thing that mattered was that they shouldn't figure out what she was up to!

With a determined look on her face, Monica turned on her heel and disappeared inside the library.

* * *

Casey and Jo stamped the snow from their boots and entered the front lobby.

"Some detective you are," Casey teased. "We should have gotten here hours ago!"

"Can I help it," Jo answered, "if I have a tribe of sick little siblings to take care of? They all have colds and everybody needed something—help with homework, a spoonful of medicine, a chest rub . . ."

"Well, we're here now, but I hope we haven't missed Monica and Derek," Casey said.

Monica was sitting with a book in front of her at one of the round oak library tables when her friends wandered into the reading room.

"There she is!" Jo whispered to Casey. "She really is here."

"Where did you think she'd be?" Casey asked.

"She's not with Derek, though," Jo observed. "Hmmm."

They walked over to Monica, who looked up and seemed quite startled to see them.

"Oh, hi, you guys," Monica said with a smile. "What a surprise! Have a seat and join me."

"What are you doing here every night?" Casey asked bluntly.

"Um, I like it here. It's peaceful." Monica smiled again. "It's a nice place to get studying done."

"Really?" Jo asked. "Your mother told me you come here every night with Derek Stone."

"Oh, well, sometimes. As you can see, he's not here now. Sometimes I like to come alone," Monica said.

"But Monica . . ." Casey frowned. "We're supposed to be your best friends. How come you never told us about this library business?"

Monica looked flustered for a moment. "What's to tell?" Then she grinned. "I suppose I didn't want you to think I'm turning into a bookworm or a nerd or anything."

"We *know* you're not a bookworm or a nerd," Jo said shrewdly. "You could have mentioned that you just happen to like the library!"

Monica let out a deep sigh. "Why do I get the feeling that you're grilling me?" she asked.

"You're right, Monica." Casey sat down and slipped out of her jacket. "We are grilling you. We've been suspicious lately because it seemed as though you were hiding something from us."

"You seem really nervous," Jo said, also sitting down beside Monica. "You know, spacey, ditzy. Not like the Monica we've always known and loved."

Monica chuckled. "Well, as you can see, here I am. I don't have any big secrets. Maybe I've just been nervous about my uneven bars problem."

"You say you have no secrets?" Jo raised one eyebrow and stared at her friend. "How about a certain new kitten in your house?"

"Yeah," Casey echoed. "What about that? You never told us Derek gave you a kitten."

But Monica didn't seem to notice her friends were hurt. She merely shrugged. "I was planning to surprise you when you came to my house the next time," she said.

"I'll bet," Jo mumbled under her breath.

Casey was the first one to soften. "Look, Monica, we're sorry. We shouldn't be so suspicious."

Jo kept staring at Monica. She didn't want to miss a single detail. "Tell me one thing," she said slowly. She reached out and took the book that lay open in front of Monica. "When did you get interested in *kidney surgery*?"

"You gotta be kidding," Casey murmured, looking at the book.

Monica looked blank at first. Then her eyes lit up. "So you caught me," she said.

"At what?" Jo pressed.

"At my secret ambition. I think I've decided to become a surgeon—after I go to the Olympics, that is. This stuff is *so* fascinating," she told them.

"Come on, Monica. You actually like reading about organs and blood and junk like that?" Jo inquired. "I thought you hated going to the doctor."

"You can't even dissect a frog without causing major malpractice!" Casey pointed out. "And algebra is your worst subject."

"Nevertheless." Monica smiled at them. "We have to start thinking about the future. I'm going to start looking for colleges with good premed programs," she announced.

Jo glared at her friend. Things just didn't add up. It felt like a puzzle with a missing piece. Jo knew Monica wasn't at the library to read up on surgery. And why wasn't Derek there if she had left the house with him as Mrs. Wright had said? Had Monica and Derek had an argument? Jo just couldn't put her finger on what was wrong.

Much later that night when she was almost asleep in her bed, Jo recalled the whole library scene as clearly as if she were looking at a movie in slow motion.

It wasn't that glib story about keeping a kitten a surprise that was so strange. It wasn't even the fact that Monica had pretended to be reading a medical textbook. No, it had something to do with Monica's arm.

Monica had been holding her wrist in an odd, strained way. Her face had been pinched with pain. She'd been trying to hide the fact that her wrist really hurt.

And Jo intended to find out *why*.

The next morning, Monica arrived at school with her wrist all taped up. She'd been to the doctor for an early-morning visit, and she managed to slip into homeroom just as the final morning bell rang.

She was so nervous she could feel her heart racing. If they were going to finger her and Derek, they'd probably do it right away, that morning. She remembered, from reading detective novels, that culprits were usually caught in the first twenty-four hours or not at all. After a day or so, the trail tended to get cold.

Please, please, let the trail be cold, she thought, closing her eyes for a second.

A crackle of static came over the public address system just then. Every morning during homeroom the principal made half a dozen announcements to the students—usually very boring ones. Today, however, his news was not boring.

"I have a most serious infraction of the rules to report," he began.

Monica heard his deep, angry voice and shivered. She wanted to slip underneath her desk and disappear.

"What now?" Rachel, the girl next to her, whispered. "Somebody wrote on a bathroom wall?"

"There was a break-in here last night," the principal went on in his serious tone.

At that, Rachel and several others in the classroom whistled. This was no small matter!

Monica gripped the edge of her desk tightly with her fingers. She was afraid if she let go, she'd go running out into the hallway like a crazy person and confess to the whole world. Was he going to mention her name, or Derek Stone's? She had to stay cool!

"We're glad to report that nothing was stolen," the principal continued. "But this is a most serious offense, and we have reason to believe the break-in was the work of a student."

Rachel leaned over toward Monica. "Why would anyone want to break into this stupid place?" she asked. "I'd rather break *out*!"

"Right," Monica agreed. She managed to smile thinly. She wondered what Derek was doing right this minute and what kind of mental agony he was going through.

Then it hit her—the principal was finished talking about the break-in. He was going on to talk about SATs and PSATs, and the topic of the break-in had been dropped, at least for now. There had been no mention of the gym or the balance beam—or the flashlight! Monica breathed a small sigh of relief. Maybe it was all going to be okay. Maybe the principal was only trying to throw a scare into the students, and nothing more. Maybe they wouldn't even bother looking for evidence in a small-potatoes case like this.

Monica decided that if she just stayed calm, she would get through this. It wouldn't be easy to do with both her wrist and her stomach hurting, but she could make it. She had to!

At practice that afternoon it seemed to Monica that Bear Benson was staring extra hard at all of his team members. Was it just her imagination or was he studying the girls, one by one?

"Monica!" Bear called out to her as she sat on the side bleachers watching the others practice during a short break.

"Yes, sir?" she leapt up and went over to him.

"You have your wrist taped," he observed.

Her pulse quickened. "Yes. I fell—on a sidewalk—and I had Dr. Burney look at it this morning."

"And? How is it?" Bear asked.

Monica felt like an amoeba under a microscope. Bear was looking at her so carefully, in such a suspicious way!

"Dr. Burney said I ought to rest it for a day, but he's almost certain I can be in the Carlton meet," she told the coach.

As Bear continued to stare at her, she began to feel a chill along her spine. "Hmmm. So you fell on a sidewalk? Where?"

"Outside the public library. Last night," she explained.

"Outside the library? At night?"

"Yes, coach."

He frowned. "It's not like you to be clumsy, Monica."

She prayed that her hands wouldn't tremble, now of all times. "There was some snow, and it was dark. I guess I slipped on a patch of ice," she lied.

He appeared to think the situation over carefully. "Well, I guess you'll have to sit out the rest of practice today. Why don't you stay and watch, though, anyway?"

"Yes, sir," Monica answered automatically. "I will."

Finally, Bear nodded his head, as though he'd said all he'd planned to say. "Hope you'll feel better soon," he said. Then he turned and walked over to the vault.

I'm making a vow right now, Monica thought, pressing her hands against each other so they'd maybe stop their frantic shaking. *If I get out of this mess . . . And maybe I don't deserve to, but if I do, and they don't kick me off the team . . . then I'll never try another thing that's against the rules!*

Her eyelids fluttered closed for a brief second. *And I'll never, never tell another lie as long as I live!!* she swore to herself.

"Are you okay, Monica?" Jo suddenly asked.

"Oh, sort of." Monica opened her eyes and managed somehow to smile at her friend. "It's just that my wrist hurts today."

"Yeah, I noticed that. I've been wondering all day why you didn't tell us about it last night," she said.

"It didn't seem like much, then," Monica said. "It hurt a little, but I figured the pain would go away in a couple of hours."

Jo stared at her. "But why didn't you say something if it hurt?"

"Jo, you're grilling me again," Monica snapped. "Why? Do you think I'm some sort of criminal, or what?"

"Of course not." Jo was quiet for a moment. "Sorry, Monica." She put out a hand to touch Monica's shoulder. "I guess you're entitled to your little secrets, if you want."

"I don't have any little secrets!" Monica blurted out.

"Okay. Have it your way." Jo still didn't seem convinced, but she looked as though she might back off for a while. "I've got to go. My turn on vault."

Monica was getting very tired of telling lies. It was so hard to remember all of them! She recalled a small poem by Sir Walter Scott she had studied in English class in eighth grade:

"Oh, what a tangled web we weave,
    when first we practice to deceive . . ."

Monica briefly wondered if Derek was going through the same thing at his practice. She hoped not. She hadn't meant to get either of them in trouble!

That night at the Benson dinner table, Bear passed the bowl of carrots to his younger daughter and asked, "Casey, did you see Monica last evening?"

Surprised, Casey looked straight into her father's

face. "Sure, Dad. She was at the library. We all were," she informed him.

Her older brother, Tom, snorted. "Is this the new craze?" he teased. "All the little freshman girls go to the library to appear studious? Come on, you probably go to check out the guys."

"Tom, we only went once!" Casey shot back.

"Did you see Monica fall?" Bear asked quietly.

Casey was shocked that her father was asking such odd questions about Monica. "No," she answered. "Why?"

"Yes, what's wrong, dear?" Mrs. Benson asked.

"I don't know if anything's wrong, exactly." Bear shook some Italian dressing onto his salad. "One more question. Is Monica seeing any special boy these days, Casey?"

Casey wasn't sure how to answer that one. She wouldn't lie to her dad, but she didn't like her father to use her as an information service, especially against either of her best friends! "Monica doesn't really date, Dad. Her parents probably wouldn't allow her to go out on a real date," Casey explained.

"I noticed she was talking to Derek Stone the other day," Bear said. "Are they friends?"

Casey squirmed in her chair. "Oh, sort of. Monica did skate with Derek last week at the rink, but that's about all it amounts to."

"I see. Thank you," her father said. His face was unreadable. But he wasn't in what Casey would have called a great mood. He seemed angry, almost. Casey felt a rush of confusion and concern. What in the world was going on?

Chapter 10

★★★★★★★★★★

THE big school bus lumbered to a stop in front of Carlton High School on Friday afternoon. A riotous roar erupted from the gymnasts inside the bus.

"Oh, we're from Fairfield High, and no one can be prouder, and if you cannot hear us . . . we'll yell a little louder!"

It had been Jill Ramsey's idea to make lots of noise when they arrived at the rival school. It was a sneaky way to psych out the other team, and it made for great Fairfield team spirit.

The bus was crowded today, with both the girls' team and the boys' team. The guys weren't competing this time, but their coach, Coach Kramer, had wanted them to go along to cheer on the girls.

Monica had had a strange week. She hadn't been able to work out with the team for the past two days because of her wrist. She also hadn't been able to see or talk to Derek, not since the night they almost got caught and then parted at the library. She understood why he was avoiding her, but understanding didn't make it any easier.

Now today on the bus, Derek still carefully stayed away from Monica. She sat with Casey and Jo on the long trip to Carlton. But finally she couldn't stand the suspense anymore. She ripped a small sheet of paper from a notebook in her gym bag and wrote a short note: "I've been so scared! How is it going so far?"

She was able to slip the note to Derek in the confusion of the kids yelling their cheer. He read it and pressed his lips together, as if to say, "Can't talk now."

When the gymnasts had finished their rowdy cheering, Bear raised his arms high, calling for silence.

"I'd like an orderly group going in, please," he requested. "Please behave appropriately at all times."

"Yes sir, Coach!" called out one of the senior boys.

Bear continued, "Now, I want you girls to make Fairfield proud of us . . . and I want you boys to be their cheering section, just as they'll be doing for you in your next meet."

"You've got it, Bear!" another boy cheered.

"So march in there with your heads held high," Coach Benson said. "Girls, let's show them how good we are." He raised his arms above his head. *"We're going to win!"*

"Right on! Yayyy!" The yell went up again, filling the bus with cries of enthusiasm. Everyone stood and started gathering their gym bags.

In the rush and noise, Derek somehow managed to move close to Monica. He whispered, "Nothing's happened yet about my flashlight. I can't understand it."

"Maybe we're safe, then," she whispered back. But she didn't actually believe it, and she could see that Derek didn't, either. He looked as if he hadn't slept in days. Monica's heart twisted when she realized what he must be going through. And all because of her!

She could feel tension beginning to knot up all her muscles. This would never do. She'd worked so hard to be prepared for this Carlton meet, she couldn't blow it by being nervous and guilty! She just couldn't!

Concentrate, Monica. *Focus.* She smiled faintly as she gave herself a pep talk. *You're going to be one of the best all-around gymnasts in today's meet!*

"Hey, Monica, you're grinning," Casey said happily. "Does that mean your wrist is better?"

"Yes, much better," Monica was glad to be telling the truth for once. Her wrist had stopped hurting, miraculously, although she was leaving the tape on for extra protection.

Once inside, the boys went on to the gym while the girls filed into the visitor's locker room. Casey was still right beside Monica.

"It's strange how my dad kept asking me questions about your injured wrist," Casey said. "I felt funny. I don't want to give out information about my best friend! I don't care if the coach is my father, I'm not his information source."

Monica felt a wave of shock go through her. "Your father was asking questions about me? What kind of questions?" she asked.

"Oh, I can hardly remember now," Casey said, frowning as she tried to recall them. "I think he asked whether you were at the library with us, and whether I saw you fall. Stuff like that."

"Oh." Monica hesitated. "You told him I was at the library with you, didn't you?"

"Of course." Casey looked at Monica as if she were out of her mind. "Because you *were* at the library with us!"

"Right." Monica told herself to relax. It didn't mean anything. No one had seen her with Derek that night and no one had any reason to think she was the culprit who had broken into the school. She even had her two best friends to back up her alibi, as it turned out.

Monica tried to ignore the rapid beating of her heart as she changed her clothes in the locker room. All of the gymnasts put on their special team leotards that were designed in blue and gold, the school colors. Monica still felt a thrill every time she slipped into hers. It was so terrific, being a member of the high school team.

And it would be so terrible if she were kicked off because of the stupid thing she had done!

She lined up with Casey, Jo, and the others by the locker room entrance to the gym. It was traditional for the team members to march out together, showing their unity and team spirit. Today they marched out to the strains of a patriotic march because their team manager had set up her tape player right near the balance beam.

Monica tried not to look at the judges' table. She knew she had to think only of her upcoming performances. She could be reasonably sure she'd do well on floor exercise, because that was her specialty. As for the rest, that would remain to be seen.

She spotted Derek up in the bleachers with the rest of the boys' team. She didn't even dare wave to him, but she felt his eyes on her. She knew he was wishing her well.

"Look, Brett is in the bleachers, too," Casey whispered as she stretched. Brett, Casey's friend from art class, had developed the habit of going to gymnastic meets whenever possible. He usually traveled with a cheering section, a few friends who carried helium balloons and wore Fairfield T-shirts that Brett had silk-screened himself.

All the usual excitement of a dual meet was there. The tense coaches were trying to look cool. The gymnasts, busy warming up, were getting themselves "in focus" for the competition. The judges, of course, sat at their table looking noncommital but very, very observant. All the gymnastic apparatus was set up in a perfect blueprint so that the gym was one giant, buzzing athletic arena.

Monica concentrated on her warm-ups, feeding herself positive messages. She listened to Bear's pep speech and gave the high-five handclap to her fellow teammates. And then it was time for the rotations.

As it was set up, Monica had the floor as her first event. She whizzed through her routine with great energy, like a triumphant, tumbling ballerina—it was the perfect way to start off the meet for her.

Next, Monica had to face the hurdle of the uneven bars. Now she held her breath. This could go either way!

But amazingly, she found herself full of confidence. She had unusual strength as she began her swing from the low bar to the high. She was supple and sure. Her leg form was perfect. She realized that those two nights of extra practice, even if they were illegal, had helped her a lot.

Her wrist hurt every once in a while, but not enough to keep her from a great exercise. On the whole, she flew through her routine on the bars with very little pain—and no mistakes! She dismounted with a high flyaway off the top bar and landed with no extra steps. She raised her arms above her head and let a smile spread across her face. She had come through!

"That was incredible," Jo said as Monica walked off the mat and grabbed her face towel. "Look at your score! Eight point eight!"

"And you were worried about your performance on bars." Casey gave Monica a congratulatory hug.

"How did you improve so much?" Jo asked.

"Just good luck," Monica said with a shrug.

Did Monica imagine it, or was Jo looking at her suspiciously? Monica shook her head. She had to stop this. She was seeing things everywhere. She thought that Bear Benson was staring at her, too, looking perplexed by her outstanding work.

At the end of the afternoon when they announced the winners of the All-Around competition, Monica was thrilled to be listed as sixth. Not bad for a freshman girl, she thought, not bad at all!

Jo came in third, and Casey got second place, which was incredible! Monica was glad to see Bear Benson give his daughter a V for victory sign. Approval was something Casey badly needed from her father every now and then.

The meet was a close one, but in the end Fairfield High rallied to a victory over their big rival.

"We did it, we did it, we did it!" the Fairfield girls shrieked. They fell into each other's arms, hugging and crying and, at the same time, laughing hysterically.

"You were great!"

"No, you were better!"

"Your vault was beautiful this time—"

The compliments resounded in the Carlton gymnasium. It was a wonderful, triumphant time ... and Monica wondered why she wasn't enjoying it more. She had done really well, hadn't she?

Bear came up to Monica and put his hands on her shoulders. "I'm proud of you, Monica," he said in a quiet, thoughtful voice.

"Thank you," Monica said shyly. Her pulse began racing double time.

"Glad to see you pulled out of that slump," the coach went on. His eyes seemed to be a glacial blue at the moment. Monica had never seen such a cold shade of blue!

"I'm glad, too." She looked away from his eyes. "I was really lucky."

Bear kept staring at her. "When was that slump—only last week? Well, you certainly improved a great deal since then."

"The whole team was great," Monica said quickly.

"Yes, they were." Bear scratched his head, looking befuddled. "Did I tell you yet that I'm taking the whole group out for a celebration pizza dinner?"

"Wow, that's super!" Monica blurted out. "Why don't I go to the locker room and tell the others?"

She hurried away as fast as she could. Once inside the locker room she stopped dead in her tracks. She pressed her back against the cold cinder block wall and just stood there, taking long, deep breaths.

This was crazy. She had such a guilty conscience that it was taking over her whole life. She was even beginning to be terrified of her own coach—a man she had known for years!

How long, she wondered, could she go on like this?

"We'll have that Super Disgusting Special with all the junk on it," Casey announced. "Sausage. Mushrooms. Pepperoni. Onions. Whatever you've got!"

"And diet ginger ales all around," Jo added as the waitress wrote down their order. Even though she loved to eat, Jo was the one who never forgot that they all had to watch their calories if they wanted to be just as good in the *next* meet.

The Pizza Palace in Fairfield seemed noisier than it had ever been, filled with the victorious girls' team and the members of the boys' team, too. The group was giddy with success—and hungry, too.

"That's funny," Jo said to Monica. "How come Derek is sitting at the other end of the table? He could sit here with us. Did you two have a fight?" she asked.

"Oh, no. He's just sitting with his friends." Monica shrugged. The truth was, she and Derek still didn't want to be seen together, but she couldn't tell Jo that. Jo was already acting so suspicious, asking her questions like that all the time! "Besides, there's nothing for us to fight about," she hurried to explain. "We hardly know each other well enough to fight, Jo."

"I see," Jo said slowly. But it was obvious that she didn't understand. "If there's nothing wrong between the two of you, then why don't you lighten up?"

"Okay. You're right. This is a happy occasion." Monica made a big effort to smile brightly.

"That's better! That looks more like the real Monica," Casey commented. "We were beginning to think that some aliens came and stole you away."

"They did. They left an android in my place. I am the computerized gymnast. I have been programmed to perform like Mary Lou Retton even though I am too tall," Monica joked in a nasal voice, and the whole group started laughing.

In the midst of the laughter, something down at Derek's end of the table caught Monica's eye. She turned and saw the coaches of both the boys' and the girls' teams talking to Derek with serious expressions on their faces.

Monica felt a cold chill run down her spine. Why would both coaches want to talk to Derek at one time? She watched as they asked Derek to come along with them. He stood up, looking frightened, and followed the coaches to a table on the far side of the restaurant.

"What's going on?" Jo whispered. "Is Derek in some kind of trouble?"

"How would I know?" Monica answered. The noise in the pizzeria suddenly seemed to be magnified to a roar in Monica's ears. She strained the muscles of her neck, trying to see what was happening at that table with Derek and the coaches.

She didn't have long to wait. First, Monica saw that Coach Benson was holding the flashlight that Derek had lost on Tuesday night in the gym. Bear placed it on the table right in front of Derek. She saw Derek's face twitch with fear, and she wanted to run over there and protect him from what was coming.

"Derek looks scared enough to have a coronary," Casey noted, sounding worried. "I wonder what they're saying to him."

Monica swallowed hard. "Your dad never mentioned anything about this—about Derek or—anything?"

"No. Well, maybe once." Casey frowned. "But I

can't imagine what would make them all look so grim and angry!"

"I wonder what the flashlight is for?" Jo mused, also straining her neck to see.

Monica continued to watch, though she pretended to be looking at the mirrored walls and the potted palm just beyond the frightening scene. Her heart was twisting with sympathy for Derek—and also with fear for herself.

Then she saw Derek change his expression. She saw him looking almost relieved, as if he were getting something over with.

He's confessing, Monica realized.

Chapter 11

★★★★★★★★★★★

FROM across the room Monica watched as Derek nodded his head to everything the coaches were asking him. When, she wondered, would he tell them the part about her? Then she'd be in disgrace, too, and kicked off the team, and who knew what else . . .

But that didn't happen. Derek finished talking, the coaches conferred privately off to the side, and then the matter seemed to be settled—at least for the moment.

Monica felt a tight pressure in the back of her throat. She was really confused!

Within minutes Coach Kramer had led Derek out of the pizza parlor. That left the rest of the kids to speculate about what was going on.

Bear Benson came back to their table and raised a hand, as if he planned to make an announcement.

A hush fell over the table. Everyone stared expectantly at Bear.

"I might as well tell you people what happened," Bear said in a weary, disappointed voice. "Because of some incriminating evidence, Derek Stone was implicated—and has just confessed to breaking into our school this week."

No one spoke, or even breathed. Monica felt her heart plummet toward her toes.

Bear went on, "I won't go into all the details at this point. There's more to this story than we know yet."

Louie, a member of the boys' team, raised his hand. "Is Derek suspended from the team?" he asked.

"The jury is still out on that," Bear said. "Coach Kramer is taking Derek home so that he can tell the whole story to his parents."

Monica's stomach constricted with pain. Derek's parents! They would be so disappointed in him.

"Here's our pizza," Jo said cheerfully as the waitress brought the big Italian pie and propped it on a stand in front of them. "Well, we might as well eat this. I mean, we all feel bad about Derek, but why did he ever do such a weird thing?"

"You look sick, Monica," Casey observed. "Are you?"

"No. Or yes. I guess I am, sort of."

"Because of what happened to Derek?" Jo asked. She was cutting up the pizza and plopping it onto paper plates.

Monica nodded. Her heart was so heavy she could hardly speak. "He's such a nice guy." Somehow she managed to force the words past a giant lump in her throat.

"Do you know anything at all about it, Monica?" Casey asked.

"No," Monica said glumly. *Only everything.*

"Well, do you want any pizza?" Jo asked.

"Not right now, thanks." Monica knew she couldn't manage even one bite of that Super Disgusting Special. Her stomach hurt, and she knew now it was all because she felt so devastated about Derek.

She sat back in her chair, trying to think. It was no use. Her brain was a wild jumble of conflicting emotions.

She knew she'd have to confess, too. She didn't want to, but they would probably catch her anyway. It would be better if she said something first . . .

Well, she didn't have to decide right this minute. Tomorrow was Saturday, and there was nothing going on except Casey's slumber party later in the evening. Monica would have to find a way to talk to Derek. Together they could decide what strategy to use.

The first thing Monica did on Saturday morning was call Derek's house. Luckily, he himself answered the telephone.

"Monica, hi," he whispered hurriedly. "I'm not allowed to talk to anyone."

She let out a little moan. "You're in a lot of trouble, then?"

"Don't worry about it," he said rapidly. "Listen, I do need to talk to you, Monica, but I can't leave my house. I'm super-grounded. Probably for life."

"Oh, Derek, I'm so sorry!" Monica wailed.

"Look, we don't have much time, not for apologies or anything else," he said softly.

"Okay. What do you suggest?"

"At exactly eleven," he said, "I'll go out and start raking leaves in my backyard. There's a bunch of trees out there, a little patch of woods. Do you think you could hide out in the woods so I can talk to you?"

Monica didn't hesitate at all. "Yes, of course, I'll be there," she assured him.

"I can't blow up even one more balloon," Jo protested loudly. She and Casey were up in Casey's room, making final preparations for the slumber party to be held that night at the Bensons' house.

"Of course you can," Casey told her, handing over six more pink balloons.

"No, I'm having a serious oxygen deficiency. And besides," Jo said, "why should you be doing the decorating for your very own birthday party?"

Casey laughed. "Because. Monica was supposed to be here to help with all this, but she must have forgotten."

"Why? What did she say?" Jo stretched out on Casey's bed on the rose comforter and stared up at the poster of Mary Lou Retton on the wall. She began to blow up another balloon.

"She wasn't home," Casey explained. "I called and her mother didn't know where she had gone."

Jo stopped blowing the balloon and let all the air come zooming out. The balloon went flying around the room for a moment, then dropped onto

the floor. "Don't you think that's rather strange—
that Monica forgot her promise to you?" she asked.

"Are you going to start that again?" Casey
looked indignant. "Monica thinks we're always
picking on her."

"Well, but where is she? She usually tells someone where she's going on Saturday. Especially her
mother!" Jo pointed out.

"Yeah, but maybe she wanted to get a special
birthday gift for a certain someone we know.
Someone important," Casey quipped.

"Get real, Casey. She was a regular space-brain
last night after the meet. You saw her!"

"Yeah. She didn't eat a thing, did she?" Casey
asked.

"She didn't even know her own name, if you ask
me!"

"I wonder why," Casey mused.

"How about if we put two and two together?"
Jo said. "The secret of the kitten, then the library
dates . . . and now she falls apart when Derek's in
trouble."

"So what does two and two add up to?"

"That's just the trouble," Jo admitted. "I don't
know. Maybe she's really crazy about him, in spite
of what she says."

"It's possible," Casey said. "But Monica always
tells us everything about guys."

"I know. This isn't like her at *all*," Jo observed.

"Well, I thought we were going to leave Monica
alone," Casey reminded Jo. "She'll tell us what's
going on when she feels like it. We have to give
her *some* room."

"I guess," Jo grumbled. "But when is she going to let us in on the secret?"

"Pssst!" Monica hissed.

"Where are you?" Derek stood still in his backyard, rake in hand, a huge pile of autumn leaves stacked up next to him. He looked around, but couldn't seem to locate the source of the sound.

"Pssst, I'm over here," Monica called out in a hoarse whisper. She'd stationed herself behind a huge oak tree, hoping Derek's parents couldn't see her. Most of the snow had melted, but the morning was crisp and cold with a wind that seemed to penetrate even the warmest jacket. Monica had worn autumn colors, brown and gold and orange, hoping to camouflage herself among the trees.

Derek sauntered nonchalantly toward her hiding place. If anyone had been watching, he merely appeared to be inspecting the lawn over near the woods. He didn't look in Monica's direction, even when he was only a few feet from her.

"Thanks for coming," he said in a low voice.

"Did you think I wouldn't?" she asked, amazed. "I feel so awful about what happened to you."

"I told you to forget about that." Derek moved closer and started to rake again. "Listen, Monica, I've decided something."

Monica was almost afraid to ask what he meant.

"I'm never going to tell them about you," he announced firmly. "And I don't want you to say a word, either."

"What!" She was stunned, almost speechless.

"Look, what's the point?" Derek argued. "I can keep telling them I did it on my own."

Derek barely moved his mouth as he spoke. His eyes were on the ground where he was idly scratching at some leaves with the rake. "They don't really believe me because they saw all those footprints in the snow, but they can't prove anything."

"Derek, no. Why should you take the rap? No," Monica insisted.

"Listen to me." He took a chance and faced her directly. There was a pleading look in his eyes. "I've thought about this. You happen to have a lot of ability. You're really dedicated to gymnastics. I think you'll be a great gymnast someday."

"Derek, that doesn't have anything to do with this."

"Yes, it does. I want you to stay on the Fairfield team and not get into any kind of trouble. Do you understand?" he asked.

Monica nervously chewed her lower lip, torn with wanting to agree with him and yet knowing that it was wrong. "No. No, I don't. You'll be kicked off your team—"

"It doesn't matter," Derek interrupted. "I've been losing interest in gymnastics anyway . . . well, sort of." He hesitated before he went on. "I love to watch you, Monica." He turned shy suddenly and looked down at his foot. He coughed nervously.

"Derek, what you're suggesting just isn't possible. I couldn't live with myself if I let you take all the blame," Monica told him.

"Monica, you don't understand." Derek paused

again. "I've had a crush on you for a long time," he finally said.

That came as no surprise to Monica, but she couldn't help but be affected by his confession. It was so sad that such an emotional moment had to take place under such terrible circumstances!

"Derek, that's really sweet of you," Monica said. She smiled at him. "But there's a lot more to this! For one thing, do you realize that Coach Benson suspects all the girls on my team of the break-in?" she asked.

Derek looked up for a minute into the blue cloudless sky as if he was thinking the whole thing out carefully. "I know. They figured out right away that a girl had to be involved."

"Because of the beam," Monica said, nodding her head.

"But they can't prove anything," Derek said quietly. "If we both keep quiet, you can be in the clear."

Monica didn't answer for a while. She was so, so tempted! But she didn't want her friends on the girls' team to be under suspicion, either. The whole thing was nerve-wracking. She was positive she ought to confess and just get the ordeal over with.

"I don't think I can do it your way, Derek," she said with a heavy heart. "I have to come clear. It was my idea, anyway. *You* shouldn't suffer."

"Come on, Monica." Derek turned toward her. "Please? I want to do it this way! I care for you a lot and—"

"Derek!" Mr. Stone called out angrily from the back porch. Monica shrank back behind the big oak tree. "What are you doing? You haven't raked at all!" he yelled.

"Okay, Dad. Here I go!" Derek called loudly to his father. "You'd better take off, Monica," he whispered. "I'll see you in school. We'll talk—but not for a long time. They might be watching us."

"Derek . . ." Monica's eyes misted over and she felt a rush of sorrow and confusion. How could such a great friendship end like this? Everything was ruined, especially Derek's future in gymnastics.

She bundled her long scarf around her face and whispered, "Goodbye, Derek. I'll miss you."

But she was talking to thin air. Derek was already halfway across his backyard, chasing autumn leaves.

At home, Monica pulled Butterscotch into her arms. The kitten had been sleeping in his makeshift cardboard-box bed in the kitchen.

"You're the sweetest thing that ever happened to me," Monica whispered to her new pet. "I wish the rest of my life could stay just as safe and innocent as you."

Butterscotch looked up at her with big, green eyes and purred. His golden fur was so beautiful, with spots of white and soft brown here and there. Monica found it soothing just to hold the kitten and not think about her problems.

The problems wouldn't go away, though. They kept flying into her brain like a swarm of bees, all stinging and persistent. It was a bizarre feeling.

Finally she came to the conclusion that she

would do nothing over the weekend. She'd go to the slumber party and try to enjoy the evening, for Jo's and Casey's sakes. Then on Monday she'd talk to Derek in school, no matter who saw them together. It didn't matter anymore. She'd have to come to some sort of decision when they had their next discussion.

"I don't know if I *can* go along with what Derek wants to do, even though it's tempting," Monica whispered to the kitten.

The telephone rang, but Monica didn't get up to answer it. Her mother called from the living room. "Monica! Casey is on the line."

Monica picked up the extension in the kitchen. "Hi, Casey," she said glumly. "Happy Birthday!"

"Thanks a lot, but where on earth have you been?" Casey called out in a loud voice.

"Why?" Monica frowned at the odd tone her friend was using.

"Did you *forget*?" Casey demanded.

"What?"

"Jo's right. You *are* turning into a space case!" Casey giggled. "You're supposed to be here helping me with this birthday party!"

Chapter 12

●★★★★★★★★★★●

"I DON'T know if you should go to that slumber party, Monica," Mrs. Wright said a short while later. They were in the kitchen, and she was stirring a large pot of beef stew on the stove.

"Huh? Why not?" Panic seized Monica. Had her mother noticed how spacey and upset she was, too?

Mrs. Wright put her hand on Monica's forehead. "Because you look sick to me, dear. It doesn't feel like you have a fever, but—"

"I'm not sick, Mom, honest," Monica protested. But just saying the word *honest* made her wince. She felt as though she no longer knew the meaning of honesty!

"Well, you don't look like your usual self." Mrs. Wright stared at her daughter with concern. "Is something bothering you, honey?"

"No," Monica lied.

"Are you sure? Something about school? Or friends?"

Standing there in the warm, comfortable kitchen,

Monica was tempted to tell her mother everything, the whole sordid story. She wished she could be a little girl again and have Mommy make all the monsters go away . . .

But something held her back. Maybe it was the fact that she was grown up now and responsible for her actions. Her mom was more likely to blame *her* for the monsters, and rightfully so. Her parents would both be furious and ashamed of her if they knew what she had done, and how she had involved Derek.

At the moment Monica didn't want to get into all that scolding and punishment that would follow such a confession. It would all come soon enough, she thought.

Mrs. Wright touched her forehead again.

"I'm okay, really." She managed a convincing smile. "I've been working hard at the gym, but now the Carlton meet is over and tonight we'll just be celebrating!" she said cheerfully.

"I'm glad you did so well, Monica." Her mother had been very proud when she heard about the great scores. "You do have a wonderful team. You and Casey and Jo are amazing! You've turned out to be fabulous all-around gymnasts. But especially you, dear."

"Oh, Mom, you couldn't be slightly prejudiced could you?" Monica teased.

Mrs. Wright adjusted the red silk scarf around Monica's neck. "Perhaps slightly." She smiled. "I'm going to be at the next meet, believe me. Don't you have the League championship meet next week?"

"Yes." Monica thought about that. It was something else she was looking forward to—her first high school League competition. It would be grueling, but she was eager to be tested against all the best girls in their league. Come to think of it, the Leagues were another reason to consider Derek's suggestion that she not confess. He claimed he was tired of gymnastics. But Monica knew that she wanted to go on . . .

"I wouldn't miss the League championship, not for the world," Mrs. Wright said, grinning proudly. "I'll be the loudest cheering mom in the stands! I'll yell so loud you'll be embarrassed."

Monica was beginning to be embarrassed right now. She was squirming with discomfort because she knew she didn't deserve all this pride and admiration from her mother. She picked up her sleeping bag, her pillow, and her overnight bag. "Well, I'm on my way to the slumber party, Mom."

Her mother kissed her cheek, and Monica could tell, from the firm pressure of the lips, that she was still trying to determine if her daughter had a fever.

"And I *don't* have the bubonic plague, Mom!"

They both chuckled, and Monica left for the Bensons' house. She walked the few blocks slowly and kicked at the slush on the sidewalk. She needed the fresh air. She wanted to clear her head so that she could forget her problems and enjoy Casey's birthday party!

"Hey, you're the last one to get here," Casey told Monica as she opened the Bensons' front door.

"But I forgive you. As long as you're willing to make the salad."

"Me? Make the salad?" Monica was surprised. "You've gotta be kidding. My cooking skills are about as good as my frog dissection skills."

"Well, luckily we don't want a cooked salad," Casey said with a grin, waving her arm for Monica to come in.

Monica entered the Bensons' big, newly-carpeted living room. She was overwhelmed to see the piles of sleep-over gear that were stacked everywhere: sleeping bags, pillows, tape players, cassettes, makeup cases, games, VCR tapes, candy, sodas, doughnuts, bags of chips and popcorn, tins of homemade cookies.

"Hi! Looks like Pigout City around here, doesn't it?" Jo commented, greeting Monica with a friendly wave.

Monica said. "I can't imagine why we need a salad, with all this junk food."

"Because," Casey explained, "my mother is a health food freak, and my father is your coach who insists that you eat right while in training!"

Most of the girls laughed, but Monica shivered. Here she was, at the home of her coach. She had stayed overnight at the Bensons at least a hundred times before, but this time things were different. She was really confused about staying under the same roof as Bear Benson. Maybe she should have stayed home after all, and pretended to have the flu. But then Casey and Jo would have been even more suspicious, and she didn't need that.

"So ... everybody's here now!" Rachel Vale

called out when Monica walked in and the crowd greeted her. "That means it's time to party!" Someone turned on the TV to a music video station. The music that blared out was perfect for dancing, and most of the guests started bopping around.

Monica looked for a place to put down her stuff. It wasn't easy because of the piles of possessions that filled the living room. She wondered if some girls needed to bring everything they owned to an overnight, just for some sort of security.

She thought Casey and Jo had done a great job with the decorating. Balloons dangled from the ceiling, and a long HAPPY BIRTHDAY streamer was taped to the archway leading to the dining room. On the window seat the girls had piled a stack of wrapped birthday gifts for Casey. Monica added hers to it.

Then, instead of joining the dancers, she wandered out to the kitchen. Mrs. Benson was at the counter, cutting up onions and weeping.

"Are you crying," Monica asked, "or is it the onions?"

"It's the onions. But we need them for the hamburgers."

Monica pretended to be shocked. "We're actually allowed to eat beef? Are you serious, Mrs. Benson?"

"I know, I know." Donna Benson looked sheepish. "I wish I could convert everyone to tofu-burgers instead. But I have to yield to popular demand."

Monica decided that today, with the frame of mind she was in, she felt more comfortable in the kitchen with Mrs. Benson than she did out there at the party. "I was assigned to make the salad," Monica began, "so just lead me to the cucumbers and radishes."

Just then Bear came ambling into the room. "Hello, Monica," he said. Monica thought his face looked unusually controlled, as though he were holding back something he wanted to say. She tensed, feeling light-headed all of a sudden. *What did he know?*

"You don't really have to do the salad, dear," Mrs. Benson assured Monica. "I'll make it. Why don't you go and have fun with the other girls?"

"Thanks, Mrs. B. Thanks a lot." Monica quickly headed out of the kitchen. She couldn't believe she was so terrified of Bear Benson! She'd known him almost her whole life, but now he looked so cold, so calculating, so . . . suspicious. Either that or she was cracking up!

She had to do something else so she could stop thinking this way. She went over to the group of dancers.

"So. What else is on the party agenda?" she asked Casey.

"Oh, wait till you see." Casey stopped dancing. "This is really great. We have a whole stack of T-shirts and some pails of dye."

"I love tie-dying. Can I do my sweatshirt, too?" Darlene called out.

"You can all do whatever you want," Casey told them.

"Can I do my pajamas?"

"Can I make my T-shirt purple?"

Most of the girls stopped dancing and trooped out to the enclosed porch. The picnic table out there had been equipped with string, clothes pins, safety pins, and rubber bands.

The porch floor was lined with plastic tubs of dye, strange-looking brews with neat names like Red Wine, True-Blue, Aquamarine, and Mellow Yellow.

"How did you learn to do this?" Jo asked Casey.

"From Brett. You know he does silk-screening, but he dabbles in this stuff, too."

"Can we start right in?" Rachel said.

"First you want to decide what design you want." She began showing the girls how to work with the clothespins, safety pins and string.

"When you have your shirt all secured with any of these items, you wet the whole thing in a bucket of water first—like this." Casey demonstrated.

Her idea seemed to be a big hit with everyone. But Monica held back. She felt as though she were in some sort of vacuum, removed from everyone else. She could hear them having fun, but she wasn't really *there*, as part of the group. It was a weird feeling—and a lonely one.

Supper came next, a huge feast on the long dining room table. Bear had barbecued the burgers, and Mrs. Benson had fixed all the trimmings. The girls provided the appetites—and the noise.

With Bear sitting right there, Monica couldn't eat a bite.

"I guess I still have a touch of that virus," she murmured as an excuse.

"What virus?" Jo wanted to know.

"Whatever's been making my stomach hurt." Monica looked down at her empty plate. "Maybe I'll just have a hamburger roll." But when it came right down to it, she couldn't even swallow the small piece of bread. And all the while her coach sat quietly, not really staring at her, but somehow she was positive that he was watching her.

"Well, poor Monica," Casey said. "Here you were feeling sick all week, and we never knew it."

"Your friends just thought you were being secretive," Rachel said with a twinkle in her eyes. "Casey and Jo were playing detective for a while there, did you know that?"

"Oh, I know," Monica mumbled. She could practically feel Bear's eyes on her. Was he listening to everything the girls were saying? She wished the floor would swallow her up and take her far away from this party.

At last the meal was over. Mr. and Mrs. Benson began clearing the dining room table. When they announced that they were retiring for the evening, Monica began to feel that she could breathe once again.

"Now we've got something really great," Casey said. "More T-shirt stuff: it's called puff writing!"

"Are you kidding? What is it?" Everyone gathered around Casey. She took out several tubes that looked like liquid embroidery, and someone groaned in protest. "That's baby stuff."

"No, no this is neat. Watch . . ." Casey began to squeeze the contents of the tube on a big old shirt of her brother's. The pink stuff came out bright and three-dimensional, almost like toothpaste would.

"Are you sure you're okay, Monica?" Jo asked, coming up to stand beside her. "If you're really sick, I'm sure Coach would drive you home."

"No!" Monica said, with almost too much force. "I don't need a ride home," she said more softly.

"Just worrying about you, pal." Jo patted her arm affectionately.

Suddenly all the lights were turned out.

Mrs. Benson appeared in the darkened dining room carrying a huge birthday cake with brightly burning candles around the edge of it. On top of the round cake was a small figure of a girl—Casey, of course—on a balance beam made out of frosting.

"There she is, being a hotshot on the beam!" someone called out in a teasing tone. They sang the happy birthday song and clapped when Casey blew out her candles.

"Fifteen of them, now," Jo remarked. "Casey's the first one of us three to reach fifteen. How does it feel, Old Lady?"

Casey pretended to be thinking deeply. "How does it feel, how does it feel . . ." She looked around the room. "It feels like I ought to be on my way to the Olympics already!"

"You know what?" Jo said, handing Casey a knife with which to cut the cake. "I think you already are." A burst of applause followed Jo's statement.

Monica stayed in the shadows, watching the fun but unable to contribute anything. Usually Monica was the life of any party—bubbly, witty, and totally crazy. Tonight she felt more like a wet blanket.

Casey opened all her gifts, exclaiming over each one. Monica had given her a pretty cotton blouse, just perfect for a tan winter skirt she had. "Thanks a million, Monica," she said.

"You're welcome." Monica managed a smile. Her friend's birthday was important, after all, and she shouldn't be letting her gloomy feelings spoil it for Casey.

Finally, Monica decided, it was time to curl up in her sleeping bag. The night wasn't over, not by a long shot, because a bunch of girls had decided to conduct a major makeup seminar in the front hall. And there were half a dozen scary movies to be watched on the VCR.

But at least those who wanted to sleep could give it a try. Monica was exhausted from all the tension of the past week. She wanted the whole party—the whole weekend—to be over, so she could confess on Monday. Sleep sounded like a wonderful escape.

So, in the eerie music of some ridiculous ghost movie that Jo had rented, Monica snuggled down in her thick sleeping bag. She rested her head on her favorite pillow from home and closed her eyes.

She was located in between the sleeping bags of Casey and Rachel, but they were sitting up near the television, wide awake. They screeched every time some slimy hand came slithering around the corner toward the teenage actresses. The film sounded really gross, but it didn't bother Monica a bit. Minutes later, she dropped off to sleep without having to count anything.

When Monica opened her eyes, the whole Benson living room was dark and miraculously silent.

There were wall-to-wall girls in sleeping bags, and some of them were softly snoring. But at least no one was watching TV or slathering makeup on anyone else. All was peaceful.

Monica turned over, noticing for the first time that the floor was cold and hard. Even the Bensons' new carpeting didn't help. Oh, well, that's what slumber parties were all about. She closed her eyes again and tried to go back to sleep.

But she couldn't. Her mind was racing, and so was her heart.

Monica sat up, looking around to see what could be keeping her awake. But all was silent and still. The rest of the girls were sound asleep—all except Monica.

She tried again, a few more times, to drift off back to sleep. It was impossible. She had something upsetting on her mind. She'd done something she was truly ashamed of, and Derek was taking the rap, and now she was covering it up.

But for a good reason, Monica told herself. Everything I've done, and plan to do, is for gymnastics . . .

She sat up again and held her head in her hands. At times she could visualize, so very clearly, what it would be like to wear that Olympic gold medal around her neck . . . The town of Fairfield would declare a "Monica Wright Day," because they'd be so proud of their hometown girl. The marching band would be playing, the whole town would turn out on the Main Street green, and there would be Monica with sprays of flowers in her arms . . . The crowds would roar their approval as the Mayor gave Monica a gold key to the city. Patriotic fireworks would explode above Lake Michigan, telling the world that Illinois had this wonderful, amazing gold medal gymnast ... And oh, how proud Monica's parents would be!

Monica came down from her reverie with a thud. How could anyone ever be proud of her? She wasn't even proud of herself at this point!

She climbed out of her sleeping bag, agitated and unhappy. Her head was beginning to hurt and her stomach was growling. Maybe a glass of milk would help both conditions. She knew the Bensons wouldn't mind if she slipped into the kitchen and helped herself to some milk.

She tiptoed around the sleeping bodies, feeling for the wall by the kitchen. She was grateful she knew her way around Casey's house by heart because it sure was dark.

She swung open the kitchen door. It wasn't quite so dark in there. She could see the flickering of a small candle flame—

A candle flame? How bizarre.

There was a face just above the candle flame. Monica blinked. It was—Bear Benson!

He was sitting at the kitchen table with his cold blue eyes fixed on her. It was almost as if he'd been waiting up all night for her to show up!

He spoke in a low, deep voice, a voice that sent a shiver down the length of her spine.

"Hello, Monica."

Chapter 13

✶ ✶ ✶ ✶ ✶ ✶ ✶ ✶ ✶ ✶

MONICA let out a little gasp. "I . . . came to get a glass of milk," she stammered. "But it's not important . . ." She turned to go back to the living room.

"Wait, Monica," Bear said in a very authoritative tone, sounding like a school official instead of Casey's father.

"Gotta get back to my sleeping bag," Monica said quickly. "I'm exhausted."

"I said, *wait*!" Bear stood up and Monica froze in her tracks. She turned to face him. She was trembling all over.

"It's time for us to have a serious talk, young lady," He said coldly.

Then Monica noticed something that was truly bizarre. Bear Benson's eyes were *glowing*, almost like a vicious vampire in a scary movie. Monica could no longer see the pupils in Bear's eyes, because they seemed to be lit up from within his skull.

That's it, she thought. *I'm outta here!*

Without stopping to think of the consequences,

she turned on her heel and ran. She flew to the
front door, unbolted it, and slipped outside before
Bear could even leave the kitchen.

When her feet hit the frost-covered grass, she
realized that they were bare. She'd get pneumonia
at the very least—but it was worth it, to get away
from her coach! She flew across the lawn, painfully
aware that she was wearing only her pajamas. It
was freezing out here!

The light on the front lawn came on just as she
ran past it. She turned and saw Bear Benson coming down the front steps after her.

"Monica!" he called out in a creepy monotone
voice. "It's time to confess!"

No! she thought, *he's just trying to scare me! I
don't have to confess unless I want to! Derek told
me, I don't have to get kicked off the team . . .*

Bear was close behind her now, but Monica
knew a lot of great hiding places. And one of them
was right nearby—the big old forsythia bush that
stood on the property line between Casey's house
and the house next door. Winter or summer, the
bush was thick with branches and provided a private little retreat way inside. The girls used to hide
under it when they wanted to get away from Casey's brother Tom, who always tried to make life
miserable for them.

Monica slipped quietly under the foliage. She
crammed her body close against the center of the
forsythia and watched as Bear Benson went charg-
ing off in the wrong direction. She had fooled him.

She took a deep breath of the cold night air and
almost giggled with hysteria. For the moment s

was safe. But what was she supposed to do for the rest of the night?

"Running away like that!" Monica thought she heard those words spoken aloud, but she knew she couldn't have. "I don't know why you did such a crazy thing," the same voice said. She blinked. It was Derek, sitting right there under the bush, beside her!

"How did you get here?" Monica asked. Then she saw another figure in the dim light, a person in a uniform. It was Dan, the custodian from Fairfield High!

"What's going on?" Monica whispered. Her spine was crawling with a sense of horror. But her mother and father came through the branches just then, followed by all the girls on the team . . . one by one. They were all shaking a finger at her because they were deeply disappointed in her.

"Confess," the girls on the team chanted.
"Confess," said her parents with very sad eyes.
"Confess!" Dan, the custodian, ordered.
But Derek shook his head. "No, don't tell them anything."

Monica tried to let out a scream, but no sound came forth. She had no voice!

Then she woke up. *Really* woke up, still in her sleeping bag on the floor in the Bensons' living room. She was bathed in perspiration and her heart was thumping like the drums in a heavy metal band.

She looked around. Everyone else was asleep. Just as she had dreamed, there were a few girls faintly snoring. But the kitchen was in darkness and so was the rest of the house. She let out a sigh of relief. It had only been a nightmare!

She touched her forehead and felt the beads of sweat. She knew she couldn't go on this way, with her guilty conscience working overtime. Monica sat up. She had to talk to someone.

"Hey. Pssst. Casey." Monica called out in a whisper, tapping her friend's shoulder. "I'm sorry to wake you, but I need to talk to you."

"Huh?" Casey mumbled. She sat up and sleepily rubbed her eyes.

Monica stood up and tiptoed over to Jo's sleeping bag. She knew it was Jo's because she could see her blond head sticking out at one end. "Jo, hey Josie . . . Please wake up." Monica shook the sleeping bag gently.

Jo sat up, bleary and confused, just like Casey. "What's wrong?"

"I need to talk to you guys," Monica pleaded. A solitary tear rolled down her cheek. "I need your help."

Casey and Jo seemed to sense something serious was bothering Monica. They grumbled a little, but they quickly roused themselves to a standing position.

The three of them stumbled over all the sleeping bags to the kitchen, where Casey switched on the small light over the sink.

"What's wrong, Monica?" Casey asked, her eyes blinking as they adjusted to the light.

"I *knew* something was wrong," Jo said. "I knew it."

"And I told you, Monica would talk when she was good and ready," Casey added.

"I'm ready now," Monica said in a hoarse voice, another tear sliding down her cheek.

"We never suspected anything like that!" Jo said with a gasp, once Monica finished telling them the truth. "You and Derek, using the gymnastics equipment at night? That's against every rule in the book!"

"I know," Monica said glumly.

"That's horrible," Casey murmured, as if it were the worst story she'd ever heard. "You've been carrying around all that guilt and worry!"

Jo leaned forward in her chair. "Let me try to get this straight. Did you say Derek did this strictly for you? He engineered the break-in? He coached you? And now he wants to take the rap for both of you?"

Monica nodded. "Yes. But it was my idea to do it in the first place."

"Wow, what a guy," Casey said softly. "He must really be crazy about you."

Monica noticed that her friends hadn't offered any advice yet. They had listened and they had been sympathetic, but they hadn't told her what they thought she ought to do. Suddenly she had this awful premonition that they weren't going to, either.

"What do you guys think?" she asked. "Casey? Jo?"

A silence fell. Monica watched the digital clock on the microwave change to 5:06. It would be dawn soon.

"Come on, you're my best friends. What should I do?" Monica asked.

"We can't make this right for you, Monica," Jo finally said. "We'd like to, but . . . no one can solve it but you."

"But can't you just tell me what you think I should do?" Monica pleaded.

Casey and Jo exchanged glances. "We'd like to help," Casey said, "but this is too important. You have to feel right about whatever you decide."

Monica nodded. Casey was right. She had to tackle this mess all by herself—she was the one who'd created it.

"I guess I already know what I have to do," Monica said slowly. "But I am grateful to you guys for listening. It helped me sort things out."

"That's what friends are for!" Casey smiled at her.

"So have you come to a decision?" Jo looked earnestly into her friend's eyes.

"Yes." Sadly, Monica turned to Casey. "Will you ask your dad if he'll talk to me, first thing in the morning?"

Casey nodded.

"I know I might get kicked off the team," Monica said. "But I have to take my chances and whatever punishment there is."

Casey and Jo jumped up and went over to her. They embraced her in a fierce, three-way hug.

"Whatever happens, we're with you all the way," Jo said.

Casey squeezed her even tighter. "Remember, we love you, Monica . . . no matter what!"

Talking to Bear Benson the next day was the hardest thing Monica had ever done. When the coach showed up right after the big pancake breakfast Casey and her mom made for the whole crew, he looked across the kitchen, straight at Monica. Monica looked at his face and saw only the good Bear that she had always known—nothing of that evil creature in her dream!

Still, his familiar face made it all the more difficult to tell him what she'd done, because he *was* Bear, someone who had trusted her—once—and not some cold-eyed stranger.

"Could we . . . maybe . . . take a walk while we talk?" Monica asked, slipping into her jacket. Bear nodded and went for his coat and gloves.

They walked along the quiet residential streets of suburban Fairfield. Monica told the story right from the beginning, when she started to feel she was "losing it" on the uneven bars. She left nothing out, and she tried to be brutally honest about herself. She wanted Bear to realize that Derek wasn't at fault in the escapade.

When she was done, Bear, amazingly, didn't look surprised.

"I'm glad you told me all this on your own, Monica." They continued to walk as they spoke. "You know, I had my suspicions all along."

"You did?" Maybe she hadn't been paranoid,

then. Bear had really been watching her all those times! "Was it because of the two sets of footprints in the snow? Or the balance beam?"

"Both. Also, Derek isn't that enthusiastic about gymnastics, from what his coach says. We couldn't exactly imagine him breaking in to use the equipment. We knew a girl had to be involved, also. All along I had a hunch that you'd do anything to get out of that slump."

Monica didn't know what else to say. She stared at her feet as they steadily walked down the block. The morning was cold and damp, with gray skies that were clouded and somber. She wondered if she would ever stop feeling so terrible.

"Why would you ever do such a thing, Monica?" Bear asked in a pained voice.

"I know this isn't a good enough reason, but—I wanted to improve. I wanted Fairfield to beat Carlton. And I wanted to do well—for me and for the team," she told him. "I just felt like everyone was getting better, except me. And I wanted to be the best!" she said fiercely.

He shook his head. "I know you do. And winning is important, of course," he said. "But I thought I was impressing on you gymnasts that safety is the most essential thing of all! And what you did was highly unsafe."

"I know," Monica said ruefully, holding up her wrist. "It still hurts sometimes."

"You could have had a much worse injury. What you did was—was just inexcusable."

Monica nodded. "I realize that."

Bear didn't say anything for a long while. Finally, Monica couldn't stand the suspense. "What happens now?" she asked.

He looked at her and kept walking. She had to hurry to keep up with Bear's stride.

"There has to be some sort of punishment, Monica." He spoke in a sad but firm voice. "I mean, it's commendable that you confessed on your own, of course." Bear appeared to be thinking deeply. "That's going to count in your favor. But you did wait several days before saying anything."

"I'm not asking for any favors," Monica said. "I know I did something very wrong. The worst thing about it was that I caused a nice boy to get into trouble, with his family and his coach ..." She shuddered involuntarily as her eyes filled up with tears.

Bear suddenly stopped walking. "I will have to talk this over with a few other authorities, Monica," he said wearily. "But my inclination right now is to suspend you from the team."

"Suspend?" Monica wondered if she had heard right. She stared at the coach through tear-filled eyes. "Suspend? Not expel?"

Bear nodded his head. "I'm thinking of a two-week suspension. That would exclude you from the League championship meet, naturally—"

Monica's heart dropped. She had wanted so much to compete in the Leagues! But all things considered, Bear was being lenient, and fair.

"Anyway, we'll see what the principal has to say about all this," the coach finished. He sounded as if the topic was now about to be closed. He looked at her with a less serious expression.

"Monica, do you have on your running shoes?"

"Yes, sure," she answered.

"All right then. Let's do some jogging," he allowed a small smile to cross his face. "I don't know about you, but I think I could use a good workout right about now!"

"I'm with you!" she said.

As they jogged, Monica felt her ragged nerves begin to mend. She knew that what she'd accomplished this morning was no small thing. She still had a lot of problems to face: the school principal, her parents, her teammates.

But she had taken the first step, and she was starting to feel a small sense of relief.

And Jo and Casey were on her side, now. Even though she'd lied to them and sneaked around, keeping all sorts of secrets, they had been right there for her when she needed them, and they had forgiven her for acting so strangely.

She didn't know what she would do without friends like that!

Chapter 14

★★★★★★★★★★

THE League championship was held on a Saturday. Fairfield High was chosen for it because the school had one of the largest and best-equipped gyms for gymnastics in the Chicago suburban area.

That made it doubly hard for Monica to attend the meet, right in her own hometown, and not be a participant. She kept thinking of how her parents had planned to be there before she had been suspended from the team.

"Are you going to be okay, Monica?" Casey asked her as all the girls on the team worked to set up the apparatus early that morning. Every girl on the team, except Monica, would be in uniform in a few hours.

"I have no choice," Monica answered bravely. "No, really, I'll survive."

"It'll be torture for you, sitting there on the sidelines," Jo said in a sad voice. "Especially when we have to compete against that Kelli Wagner from Arnold High. You know how conceited she is!"

"She thinks she's such a hotshot on floor," Casey said. "Well, I've got news for her. Our Monica can tumble rings around her!"

Monica sighed. "Our Monica, as you put it, is not competing today."

Casey and Jo looked at her with genuine sympathy in their eyes. "At least you're still on the team. It could have been worse," Jo said.

"Sure, Monica. It could have been so much worse." Casey sniffed a little bit, as if she were holding back a tear or two. They weren't used to competing without one another.

The meet got underway with a fanfare of music and cheering. The League competition was a huge interscholastic event, with many schools participating. As team after team arrived, the Fairfield gym began to resemble an enormous three-ring circus.

Monica sat in the bleachers, feeling terribly left out. She wanted to attend the meet, of course; nothing would have made her miss the performances of her friends and teammates. But she had a feeling it was going to be torture, just as Jo had predicted.

"Hi, Monica."

She turned quickly and was amazed to see Derek Stone standing beside her. She hadn't had a chance to talk to him since the week before—although Casey had told him about what had happened with Monica.

"Can I sit down?" he asked shyly.

"Sure! What are you doing here?"

"All the guys on the boy's team are planning to be here as spectators today," he said.

"But I thought you were permanently grounded. And suspended, like me," she said.

"My grounding is almost over," he sat down next to Monica and a little flicker of a smile crossed his face. "It's nice to be able to talk to you again."

"I'm surprised you would want to," she murmured.

"I've missed you." He stared right into her eyes, as if there was something major he wanted to say. But somehow the words didn't come, and Derek just looked as if he were memorizing the features of Monica's face.

"How's the kitten?" he finally asked, looking away.

"He's wonderful." She grinned. "He prowls around like a big game hunter, and we think he's trying to learn how to hunt for mice."

"Wow. Pretty smart little guy," Derek said.

"Of course, he won't know what to do with a mouse if he does happen to spot one," Monica added. "The mice would be bigger than he is." She knew that she was chattering, but Monica went on anyway. "I'll always be grateful that I have him for a pet."

"Good." Suddenly Derek reached out and touched Monica's hand. "Look, I don't know whether we'll ever have a chance to go out again."

Monica shook her head sadly. "It will be years before my parents trust me," she said, although she knew she was doing some exaggerating. "They were so angry and disappointed in me. I can't blame them."

"We really messed up, didn't we?" Derek asked. Monica nodded.

Just then the coaches of the different high schools began to announce the names of their girls. A fanfare of music played for each gymnast, and the large audience cheered for every girl. Monica made a real effort not to let it all get her down, but it really did hurt, watching her two best friends out there.

She turned back to Derek. It helped to have him sitting next to her.

"Maybe we'll get another chance later on," Monica said to Derek. "We did have a pretty nice friendship started."

"It's been more than friendship to me," he said slowly.

"Thanks," she said. "I'm flattered."

Monica looked back at the gym floor. The top-seeded gymnast in floor exercise, Kelli Wagner, had just been introduced. She walked out into the center of the gym. Monica watched as Kelli acknowledged the judges, then flashed a confident smile to the crowd.

Derek gave Monica's hand an extra squeeze. He leaned over and whispered in her ear, "You could have blown this chick right out of the water."

Monica smiled. "That's what Casey said."

"How's that wrist doing?" he asked.

"All right. It's almost back to normal," she said.

Across the room, Casey was doing warm-ups and getting ready for her big moment on the beam while Jo was stretching in preparation for her uneven bars routine. Once in a while they looked over toward Monica.

"You know something?" Monica said. "Casey and Jo told me to use this humiliation today as a learning experience." Monica glanced down at the hand that Derek was holding. She liked feeling close to him again.

"Sounds like good advice," Derek observed.

"Yes. I had made a promise to myself anyway in the middle of all that mess," she said. "I vowed I'd never do another sneaky thing and never tell another lie as long as I live!!"

Derek laughed. "I feel the same way. It's just not worth it in the long run."

"You said it." Monica looked over at her teammates as they continued their warm-ups. "Well my friends told me to hold my head high during this meet—and that's what I'm trying to do."

"You're lucky to have such good friends," Derek said.

"I know. They've told me over and over that they're with me all the way, no matter what."

Derek nodded. "All the way to the Olympics, right, Wright?" he joked.

"Right, Stone."

From the other side of the gymnasium, two Fairfield girls in bright gold-and-blue leotards stopped what they were doing for just a second. Casey and Jo turned to Monica and gave her a vigorous thumbs-up sign.

She signaled right back to them. "Knock 'em dead, pals," she mouthed.

Here's a look at what's ahead in TO BE THE BEST, the third book in Fawcett's "Perfect Ten" series for GIRLS ONLY.

Casey groaned as she opened the front door. "Da-ad!" she cried. "Did you really have to crash our party?"

Bear Benson, the coach of the Fairfield girls' gymnastics team, was standing on the front steps, and with him was a tall, husky man with gray hair and a mustache. Jo had seen him before—at the meet that afternoon. She had noticed him just as she was about to begin her routine on the uneven bars, her favorite piece of equipment. While she chalked her hands, he had stood nearby watching her, she was sure of it. At the time, she had briefly wondered who he was, but she'd forgotten all about him since then.

Jo's mother walked into the living room, and Coach Benson began the introductions. "I'd like you to meet Boris Krensky, Mrs. Mallory," the coach said. "He was at our meet this afternoon at Winton High School, and he has some important news for you."

Mrs. Mallory looked puzzled.

Important news? What does that mean? Jo wondered.

"Casey, Monica," Coach Benson said. "I think maybe you should head on home."

"But Dad, we haven't eaten any pizza yet. The party hasn't even started," Casey said. "You can't be serious."

Coach Benson looked at the three of them sternly, the same way he did when they giggled at practice. He shrugged. "Okay. You two can stay and hear this, too, I guess. You'd find out about it soon enough anyway. But this is basically Jo's news."

"Is something wrong with the gymnastics program?" Mrs. Mallory asked as the coach and his guest sat down. "They're not going to terminate it, are they? I heard the high school had to cut back on some of the sports programs."

"No, no," Coach Benson said. "It's not that at all. Everything is fine at Fairfield. This is good news, something to get excited about."

"So what's going on?" Casey demanded. She took a bite of pizza and stared at her father.

"I don't know if you ever heard of my school, Krensky's," the stranger began. "It's in Malibu, California."

Krensky spoke with a thick foreign accent, and Jo had to concentrate to understand every word he said. But suddenly it hit her. "Of course," she said. "I remember. I didn't just see you for the first time at the meet today either. I've seen you in Gymnastics International and on TV. You're *the* Boris Krensky, the one who trained Alexandra Watson for the Olympics, aren't you?"

"You're really Boris Krensky?" Casey asked. "For real, in person? Could you show us some identification?"

"Be quiet, Casey," Monica warned.

Krensky smiled at Casey. "Right. Alexandra Watson is a wonderful gymnast. In fact you remind me of her, Jo," he said, turning back to her.

"Me?" Jo's voice came out as a squeak, and she felt her face turn red.

"Mr. Krensky is here today, Mrs. Mallory," Coach Benson said, "because he travels around the country once or twice a year looking for prospects for his school. He visits meets and observes gymnasts, and if he likes someone he invites them to enroll. It's as simple as that."

"So today, I come to Fairfield's meet," Krensky said, "and I really like what I see. There are lots of wonderful girls out there."

"Yeah, we've got a terrific tearm," Casey said, nodding her head. "Of course, we work really hard, too."

"But what Mr. Krensky really wants to say is that he wants Jo," Coach Benson continued.

"Wants Jo?" Mrs. Mallory repeated. "What does that mean?"

"I want her to come to Krensky's Gymnastic Club in Malibu, as soon as possible. That is, if you will allow her to do so," Mr. Krensky said, taking Mrs. Mallory's hand in his and patting it. "We particularly need someone with the skills she has on the uneven bars."

"Just Jo?" Not the rest of us, not me and Monica?" Casey asked, looking as stunned as if she'd just fallen off the balance beam.

"Just Jo," Bear Benson said. He smiled at his daughter and then patted her on the back. "Don't be upset, Casey. One of these days you're going to make it, too. But I think that all of us have to be really thrilled for Jo."

The blood pounded so hard in Jo's forehead that she thought she might faint. It was like a birthday and Christmas and all the other holidays wrapped into one big surprise package! Of course, she felt a little twinge of loneliness at the thought of leaving her family behind, not to mention Fairfield and Monica and Casey—and even Lance from algebra and Matt from Spanish I. But Malibu and Krensky's? It was a dream come true—no, a wish come true!